PILLAGE & PLAGUE: MOUNT OLYMPUS ACADEMY

PILLAGE & PLAGUE: MOUNT OLYMPUS ACADEMY

MYTHVERSE BOOK 2

KATE KARYUS QUINN   DEMITRIA LUNETTA
MARLEY LYNN

Little
Fish
Publishing

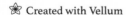

Sign up for the Mythverse Newsletter and you'll receive
THREE FREE SHORT STORIES—all set in the Mythverse!

RAGE & RUIN is part of the Mount Olympus Academy and
features Nico's mom, Maddox.

FIGHT OR SIGHT and TOOTH OR CLAW are prequels to
later books in the Mythverse series, set within Underworld
Reformatory.

1

Everyone dreams of being special in some way. Not just to their mom and dad, but to the whole world. We all believe we have something extra and unique hiding inside, just waiting to be let out. Something that's going to make your friends proud to know you, and your enemies wish they'd picked on someone else.

At three-years-old, I was convinced I was royalty. A princess specifically. I spent a lot of time waiting on the beach for my *real* mom and dad to come get me. I assumed they'd sail up to our Florida home on a tall ship, somehow fitting in the canal behind our house. They'd wear heavy crowns and beg for me to come be their princess again.

Two years later, I wanted to be a superhero. Or at least the super sidekick to my older sister, Mavis, who already was special in all the ways. Beautiful. Fastest kid on the playground. Incredibly smart. Yeah, I wanted to be special, but I knew I wasn't at Mavis' level. Just being her sidekick was a goal.

The year I turned ten was a Winter Olympics year. I fell in love with ski jumping—

a weird thing for a kid to attach themselves to, I know. My mom was way into the figure skating. She and Mavis would watch every second, picking apart costumes and coming up with their own scoring system (ranging from "Super Sucks" to "Super Does Not Suck").

"Isn't this cool, Edie?" Mavis had asked, as the endless train of beautiful girls in sparkly costumes kept going. "Way better than that skiing thing."

"Slalom," I'd corrected her. "And no, it's not way better. My people fly."

Mom had looked at me funny then, her eyebrows coming together.

"I told you raising them in Florida would make them strange," she said to my dad, who looked away from the TV a little too slowly when one of the skating girls had a wardrobe malfunction.

"Huh?" he said. "What now?"

Mom threw a piece of popcorn at him. "Your daughter wants to fly, Daniel."

"Well, I guess someone should teach her, then," he said. "I mean, how hard can it be?"

As it turns out, it's really hard. But I had to wait seven more years to discover that.

So there I was, a Florida kid who wants to be a ski jumper, with a really fast, really smart older sister.

"At least you're not totally ugly," Mavis said when I was fourteen, patting me on the head.

"But I'm not special," I said, having finally come to the realization.

Except I was totally wrong.

There *was* something inside of me the whole time just waiting to get out.

And that something was a dragon.

That's not a metaphor. I am an actual. Freaking. Dragon.

Well, not *all* the time. I'm a shifter. So sometimes I'm a dragon and sometimes I'm just normal seventeen-year-old Edie.

I gotta admit, being special—like hello I can fly and breathe fire type of special—is pretty cool. A little scary, but mostly cool. Let's see one of those figure skaters try to barbecue a bad guy—with their mouth. And those ski jumpers? They come back down. I don't have to. Not until I'm ready.

At the same time...I've lost a lot, too.

My grandma used to say, "There's always a price to pay." She'd usually say it while patting her belly after going overboard on Dad's famous key lime pie.

My grandma is dead now. She and my dad both died on the same terrible day a year ago when a rogue wave hit her condo. Or news reported it as a rogue wave, but it turned out a monster killed them. This bad dude named Leviathan.

Levi's the reason I came to Mount Olympus Academy—a school taught by actual gods. I wanted revenge. And I still do.

Now, with the whole dragon thing, getting revenge seems more possible than ever. But my teachers say I'm not ready yet. No combat missions are allowed until I officially graduate from the assassination class. We are allowed to go on reconnaissance and rescue missions, though.

And right now I'm getting ready to lead one. It's not just any rescue mission. I'm going to get my mother.

On the same day my dad and grandma were killed, both my mom and sister went missing in Greece. The gods have finally tracked Mom down and after I sorta saved the whole school when monsters invaded our Spring Fling dance, they figured it'd be okay if I went out to get her.

I shake my head, trying not to think too much about the Spring Fling. I might have saved the day, but I toasted Ocypete—my flying instructor—doing it. Actually, she was more than just a teacher. I thought she was kind of a mentor too. Someone who might take me under her wing. Literally. But it turned out she'd been a double agent the whole time she was working at the school.

Even worse, she led the monsters who attacked the night of the dance. She tried to tell me that the gods aren't the good guys, that they're only using the school and the students as shields so that they don't have to do their own fighting. But I wasn't buying the monsters as the good guys.

Not when one of them killed my dad.

2

"What are you doing?" A tiny voice squeaks near my ear.

I swat at the bat flying around my head. "Greg, we're supposed to keep a low profile and stay in human form unless there's danger," I remind my bat-shifter friend.

"I know, that's why I'm getting it out of my system before we leave campus." He lands on my shoulder. "Gotta give the wings a good flapping or else they'll be stiff the next time I use them."

He does have a point. The back problems I suffered for most of my life were from keeping my wings hidden. For pretty much my entire life I had no idea they were there. My parents thought they were protecting me by casting a spell that kept my wings hidden deep inside me. I guess it's hard to raise a daughter who's half dragon, but I still can't help but feel a little betrayed by all the lies they told me.

Once I find my mom, I'm first gonna give her the biggest hug ever (and, let's be honest, probably cry all over her too), but after that—I'm gonna have some tough questions for her to answer.

The biggest will be asking who my real parents are, or at least, who my dad is. Turns out, I wasn't entirely wrong when I was three and told my mom and dad I was waiting for my real parents to come get me. Back then, I was playing make-believe. Last year, I found out the cold, hard truth.

The parents who raised me aren't my birth parents. When I arrived at the Academy, my friend Cassie helped me discover that years ago my birth mom was a student here as well. Adrianna Aspostolos died giving birth to me. The people I thought were my parents were students here at the time, too, and my dad—a foundling who'd been raised by the goddess Themis—snuck me off campus, along with my sister Mavis.

Why Mavis and I were secrets—and in danger—I have no idea. But I bet it has something to do with who my bio-dad is.

"Oh my gods, what are we waiting for?" the constantly cranky Hepatitis asks.

I'd wanted my healer friend, Fern, to be on our team, but she and her vampire girlfriend had a really big fight about how dangerous it might be and she decided to stay behind. Hepa has actual field experience and so it was strongly recommended I choose her as a replacement. And when Themis strongly suggests something, that means you do it and you don't argue.

"Hey ladies, what did I miss?" A tall, dark, and too handsome for his own good, boy prowls toward us. Even in athletic sandals there's an unmistakable grace to his movements that hints at the panther hiding beneath.

"Um, I'm here too, Jordan." Greg pops back into human form. "I'm definitely not a lady. Not that I have anything against being a lady. I really like ladies. I'm saying lady too much, aren't I?"

"You really are," I agree.

"Oh, sorry, little guy." Jordan claps Greg on the back. "I'll try to remember your preferred pronouns for next time." Even in human form Greg is on the diminutive side, and next to the much taller and more muscled Jordan the lack of stature is even more pronounced. We all stare at Jordan. "What?" he asks. "Hot guys can be woke."

"Hi Jordan," Hepa immediately perks up, the grumpy girl I know disappearing in a haze of fluttering eyelashes.

"Hey, uh..." Jordan looks flummoxed for a second. "Chlamydia?"

"Hepatitis," I correct him quickly, before she can go for his eyes.

"Oh right, I knew it was something like that," he says, flashing a smile that makes Hepa's anger response diminish into a deep sigh. Like she might even agree that her name is an STD if he likes that better.

It's impossible to be mad at this guy. He's so friendly and open. You'd think he was a sheepdog shifter. Reaching under his shirt to scratch, Jordan asks, "Where we going again?"

An inbred sheepdog. 'Cause he's not the brightest kid at school. He is, however, the best observer in the spy class. His specialty is to park his panther butt somewhere and watch, for days if he has to. Greg insists he's never seen anyone better at concealed surveillance.

Another good thing about Jordan is he can double for a tracker, because let's face it, Greg is not great at his job. Apparently, panther shifters are natural trackers. According to Greg, Jordan is an all-around, great guy...and he'd know, since they're roommates. With Greg vouching for Jordan, I had to take him. So many people wanted to join our group —after I went all dragon at the Spring Fling I went from the loser new girl to an Academy legend.

Hepa sighs. "We went over the plan last night. There were handouts. And a PowerPoint presentation. I'm surprised she didn't cap it off with a musical number."

"Aw yeah, that woulda been solid," Jordan agrees, totally missing Hepa's sarcasm. And her point—that I am trying way too hard to be a good leader and have no idea what I'm doing.

The truth is, the last time I can remember leading anything was in second grade when my teacher would choose a different kid every week to be the line leader. The week I got chosen was Thanksgiving break, so I only got two days...and I totally got lost, too, leading the whole class into the fifth-grade wing, where we'd been intimidated by the taller, bigger, stronger kids.

And now here I am, leading a bunch of teenagers right into the mouths of taller, bigger, stronger *monsters*. That didn't work out too well at the Spring Fling, when Darcy—a merman that my best friend Cassie had a crush on—was decapitated by a centaur.

I left that part out of the PowerPoint.

Greg was friends with Darcy too. It seems like everyone was. He even tried to help me find my inner shifter once. His death was hard on us all, no one more so than Cassie. And that's why I will never accept what Ocypete told me—that the gods are the real villains.

No, Ocypete, I think. *You were on the wrong side. Not me.*

3

"Hey team!" Hermes joins us—yes, the actual god —and I stifle a groan.

Hermes was my first contact with the gods. After flirting with me more than state law allows, he gave me my first flying lesson...by dropping me from the sky.

"God-bro!" Jordan says, fist-bumping the god.

Hermes goes in for the hug, giving the panther shifter a little extra squeeze. He's a total sleaze, but at least he doesn't discriminate.

Mount Olympus Academy boasts gods for instructors, and shifters, witches, and vampires as students. While there's not exactly an interspecies dating rule, it's definitely frowned upon. Last year when Val and I—

"No," I say aloud, breaking my own thought process. I'm not going to think about Val. There's a reason there aren't any vampires on my team.

"No what?" Greg asks.

"No..." I search for an answer. Because I am definitely not *talking* about Val either. "No dance number until we come back with my mom," I finish lamely.

"Ahem," Themis is suddenly with us, her disapproving gaze falling on Hermes as he curls a tendril of Hepa's hair around one finger.

Hepa doesn't even have to slap him away. She looks him in the eye and says, "I do not consent." Immediately there's a flash of blue light where he's touching her hair, and the smell of electricity in the air.

Hermes shakes his hand but grins, undeterred. "I'm just trying to be friendly."

"Wow." I say. "You've got to teach me that spell."

"If you touch me again without my permission, I'm going to put a hex on you that will shrink your..."

"Okay, fine," Hermes tells her. True, he doesn't seem to care about the interspecies dating thing, but he could stand to discriminate a *little* bit more. We are students, after all. Hermes breaks away from Hepa, coming to me last.

"Hermes," I say, dancing out of his reach when he comes in for the hug.

"Edie," he says, nonplussed, holding his arms out wide.

Hepa's reaction has inspired me. "I don't think teachers should hug students...much less try to do other things with them."

"She means sex things," Greg cuts in.

"When are you going to learn that sex is fun?" Hermes shakes his head but drops his arms.

"Sex *is* fun!" Jordan agrees enthusiastically.

"AHEM," Themis says again, finally bringing the group into some sort of order. "Edie, is your team ready for their mission?"

I glance at the group: Jordan, still a little starry-eyed and distracted by the mention of sex; Hepa, standing at strict attention, eyes bolted to Themis; and Greg, who is looking at...my chest.

I sigh. I'd hoped he'd be over me by now. We did go to the Spring Fling together, but it was a pity date and people died, so not exactly the start of an epic romance.

"Yes," I say, trying to sound confident. At least everyone remembered their packs with their supplies. Some food, some Euros, a few other things. "We are definitely good to go."

But my voice doesn't quite ring true, because it's not.

Someone is missing.

Cassie.

My friend. The first person to welcome me to Mount Olympus Academy. The girl whose prophecies were never more relevant than the lunch menu. She also helped me find out all that information about my parents, even going so far as to touch a Seer Stone in order to increase her powers. That stone knocked something loose inside of her, causing her to see more important events. Bad events. Like when she foresaw Darcy, her crush, literally losing his head the night of the ball.

But a lifetime of saying unimportant things had sullied her reputation and she'd known no one would believe her. The last I saw Cassie she was sobbing uncontrollably near the puddle of blood that had been Darcy. I'd been shuttled away, my newfound dragon-shifting ability putting me in the spotlight. The gods all wanted to talk to the first ever dragon shifter. By the time I got back to my dorm I'd heard the news—Cassie was gone. The only thing she left behind was a note, hastily scribbled but clearly in her handwriting.

The monsters want me. They're going to take me. Send help.

I wanted to go straight out and find her, even if it meant burning down anyone who got in my way. I'd lost enough people and Cassie wasn't going to be among them. Not if I could help it. But before I could even pack my bags, Themis showed up and nixed my plan. She told me any unsanctioned mission would lead to expulsion.

I had trouble fitting in at my old school. I was pretty sure it wouldn't be any better now that I'm a dragon shifter. Plus, the Academy has become my home.

So I decided to bide my time and wait.

But Themis is still on my shit list.

Speaking of which...

Themis and her constantly judging gaze slides over my group. "A team with three shifters? And no vampire?" Her eyebrows inch higher.

"Bet I know why," Hermes adds helpfully. My temper flares, and I open my mouth, sending a small jet of fire towards him, singing his eyebrows.

"Ow! Shit, kid!" He cries, hands going to his face. "Not my money maker!"

Ocypete was right about one thing–the gods are total babies about pain. Hepa pushes past me, her hand going to her leather pouch at her side.

"I got it, I got it," Hermes waves her away, his god's blood already healing his injuries. We watch as his eyebrows grow, the bubbled skin around them smoothing back out into the chiseled features we all know so well.

"Are you done with your petty squabbles?" Themis asks me, hands on her hips.

I look at Hermes, who puts his hands up in surrender.

"Yes," I tell her.

"As I was saying, this is an interesting crew," Themis continues. Her eyes going to Jordan and Greg. "Two trackers?"

Jordan grins. "I'm not a tracker. I'm a spy. I don't conform to your stereotypes."

Okay, I don't know what the boy has been doing with his free time, with all his talk of stereotypes and personal pronouns.

Greg, noticing my surprised look, whispers to me, "Jordan got called out for being a bro so he's trying to compensate. Think he did some research when he went home for his week off...or he banged a women's studies major."

Jordan lifted his shirt after noticing the print on it and is now trying to read it upside down. He's still a bro. It's unescapable. But judging from the way Hepa is scoping out his exposed six-pack, she's definitely buying what he's selling.

"Preconceived notions of shifter roles are so last millennium," she agrees and melts when Jordan turns his grin on her.

"It's a recovery and rescue mission," I remind Themis, trying to get us back on track. "It made sense."

To me. At the time. Of course, now Themis is making me second-guess everything.

"Interesting," is all she says in the face of my carefully constructed logic.

"Alright," Themis claps her hands together. "Are you ready to depart?"

We look at one another, and nod. But Themis isn't talking to us.

"Hermes?" she asks, who seems to be distracted by Jordan's still lifted shirt.

"Huh?" Hermes asks. "Depart? Yes! I am totally ready." He jingles the key ring and the bundle of old-fashioned keys rattles. "Follow me, my lovelies."

That's right. A group of teens consisting of a witch, a bat, a panther, and a dragon are following a pervy god to an undisclosed location.

This is my life.

4

"Hold up!"

We've barely taken two steps when a booming voice stops us in our tracks. With a flash of light, Mr. Zee appears before us.

Themis audibly sighs.

"I've come to see you off," Mr. Zee says in a way that makes it clear he's doing us a great honor. "I can't let the only dragon shifter in history go off without a word of advice from me. Exceptional beings must stick together," he adds, tipping me a wink.

"Actually," Themis says, inspecting her nails. "I'm not sure that our Edie is all that exceptional."

"What?" Hermes and Mr. Zee ask...at the same time I do.

WTF, Themis? I *know* it's a big freaking deal that I'm a dragon. Everyone basically peed their pants—while fighting for their lives—when I shifted at the Spring Fling. So why is the story changing now?

Cassie's mom, Merilee, spots us as she's crossing campus, and detours to Themis' side. She looks awful, which is to be expected since her daughter was kidnapped by our enemies. Her hair is a blonde tangle and her face a shiny mess. She probably hasn't washed in days, at least not with anything but tears.

Since Cassie disappeared, I've been checking in on her mom to see how she's doing. But with planning the mission, I haven't seen her in a few days.

"Mr. Zee." Merilee tugs at his toga where it drapes over the arm. He looks down at her like one would a spider crawling on their bare flesh—with a mixture of disgust, astonishment, and certainty that he can squish her flat. Merilee, meanwhile, is oblivious to all of it. "You told me you'd have an update on Cassie."

With practiced ease, Themis takes hold of Merilee and pulls her away from Mr. Zee. "What good timing, Merilee. We were just discussing Edie's dragon status and would appreciate your historical insights."

"Yes...shifter history is endlessly fascinating," Merilee says absently.

Themis is asking her because she runs the record room. She's a seer, like her daughter, but more specifically, she's a finder. She memorizes—and mentally catalogues—everything she reads.

If it's happened in the history of Mount Olympus, Merilee knows. When I first suspected I was a dragon she laughed in my face. In a nice way. She thought the suggestion was absurd. "Dragons don't exist," she'd insisted. And up to that point, they hadn't. Until me.

So why is Themis inspecting her manicure and insisting I'm not special?

"And what did you find, Merilee?" Themis prompts.

"Oh, yes. Edie. Well, obviously you were not raised by your biological parents—"

"Hold up," Mr. Zee interrupts. "You mean, this isn't a

rescue mission for Edie's hot dragon mama?"

"No, it is not." Themis' mouth purses. "And might I remind you that your own rules state—"

Thunder rumbles the ground beneath our feet. A lightning rod appears in Mr. Zee's hand as he leans into Themis, terrifying in his rage. "Woman, thou shalt not cockblock me. As I proclaim it, so it shall be."

Themis looks more amused than scared. Still, her tone is respectful. "Of course, Zee. As you say."

"That's right." He is pacified and the lightning bolt disappears from his hand. Sunlight streams down on us once more as the clouds that had crowded overhead disperse. "Anyway," he smiles brightly, rage completely forgotten. "Those rules are for students. Parents are fair game." Mr. Zee nudges Hermes. "Am I right?"

"The fairer the game, the better," Hermes agrees.

They chuckle together. It's icky. Even Jordan looks grossed out.

Suddenly, Mr. Zee's mood shifts and he looks extremely sad. "But no hot dragon mom, huh?" he asks Themis and Merilee.

"Unfortunately, no," Merilee says, shaking her head. "Dragons don't exist, so how could one be Edie's mother?"

"But if she's not the child of dragons what is the provenance of"—he swirls a hand through the air, clearly searching for my name—"this one?"

"We believe she may be the result of a union between two shifters of different types. Perhaps a bat and an ostrich," Merilee says. "I went quite far back into the archives and found other interesting offspring—"

As soon as Merilee says archives, Mr. Zee loses interest. Or maybe he just misheard her, because he starts doing the hand jive while also humming the song from "Greece" that goes with it.

Meanwhile, Greg is ecstatic. "I knew you had some bat in you." He waggles his eyebrows. "My offer still stands if you want a little more—"

"Very little more," Hepa quietly snickers.

"An ostrich?" Jordan asks, his usual emotion—confusion —evident. "But where's the lizard part come in? Wouldn't it be like..." His forehead scrunches as he puzzles it out. "Like a bat and a Gila monster?"

"No," Themis says, very patiently. "The ostrich is descended from the dinosaurs, and some of that DNA must have been activated by the..." She actually wrinkles her nose. "By the bat, I suppose."

"Damn right," says Greg, triumphantly.

"Wait..." Jordan, even more confused, turns to Hepa. "Dinosaurs are real?"

She tries to stop herself, but the laughter erupts. I'm tempted to laugh with her, but the idea that my cool dragon might be result of an ostrich and a bat mating is a little deflating. Those are the two shifter animals I didn't want to be and now I might be both of them!

Mr. Zee crosses his arms over his chest. "I don't like all the shifters mixing. What happened to sticking to your own kind? Sure, today we've got a dragon, but tomorrow it could be a hornless unicorn."

"Um," Hermes frowns. "Wouldn't that just be a regular horse?"

"Exactly!" Zeus thunders. "That's the problem with diluting the blood."

Without saying good-bye, he stalks off, still muttering to himself about crossbreeding and well, a bunch of other stuff that sorta makes him sound like a bigot. Which is not really a comfortable thought. But I'm probably just overreacting. This is a whole different world and I am still very, very new here.

"Mr. Zee, about Cassie..." Merilee runs after him, waving her hands.

I want to go with her, to use the little bit of status I've gained to convince them we need to get Cassie. Now. But first I need to rescue my mom.

Themis clears her throat. "Edie, are you running this mission or shall we cancel so you can continue daydreaming here in the quad?"

I stare at Themis, stunned by this snark attack. "No, we're going. I mean"—I turn and gesture to the rest of the group— "Let's go team!"

Hepa rolls her eyes while Greg sends a sympathetic smile my way. When even Greg is pitying me, I know it's not going well.

Themis, Hermes, Mr. Zee, and all the other gods have this effortless attitude of power and authority. And confidence. Most of the students here do, too. They make me feel like a clueless Swamper. That's the nasty term for someone who doesn't belong. And until six months ago it's exactly who I was.

Which is why as we follow Hermes across the campus, I debate whether I should ask how we're getting to Greece. Flying—in an airplane—seems like the most obvious, but nothing at Mount Olympus Academy is that clear cut.

We're crossing the main lawn when someone taps my shoulder. Two taps, not hard enough to hurt, but definitely demanding attention.

I look over. Ugh.

With her usual "who farted" expression, Tina, my bitchier-than-thou roommate, stares at me mutely, waiting. It's possible she expects me to curtsy.

Instead I settle for a simple, "Hi Tina."

I didn't even know that she was back on campus for summer term. As usual, she looks stunning, her required uniform punked-out to her own specifications, the bright green highlights in her hair still holding their vibrance. After I saved everyone at the dance, she'd announced I was no longer the "worst person on campus," but we're not exactly besties.

More importantly...if she's here then that means Val is too.

I strain around her to look. Surprisingly helpful, Tina actually steps aside.

Then I see why Tina is being so accommodating.

Val stands with another vamp. No, not just stands. He's holding hands with her.

I feel the heat rise in my throat, but I hold it back. I do not flambé my romantic rivals.

I'd practiced acting cool and disinterested for when he returned to campus. But for some reason it never occurred to me that his fiancée would come with him. Yep, *fiancée*. Even if it's the product of an arranged marriage, seeing the two of them together is just too much. I try to step away, to continue following Hermes, to focus on my mission, but Tina grabs my arm.

"Oh, you just have to meet Val's fiancée." She loops her elbow through mine and pulls me along. Vampires are freaky strong, so I have no choice but to let her lead me. I mean, I could fry her with a blast of dragon fire, but that might get me kicked out of school.

I'd be more tempted to run the risk and set Val on fire, but the healers magicked him with a fireproof spell last year after he caught on fire for the third time, deciding to allocate their resources elsewhere.

"Edie, this is Val's soon-to-be wife, Larissa Golov, from the Russian Golovs. She transferred schools to be with her intended. And of course, you know Val. I mean, didn't you guys...date? Or something?"

"Yeah, I get it, Tina. Thanks."

We kind of dated. Val set up a fake relationship with me in order to shield me from accusations after students were being turned into piles of ash all over campus. He'd claimed to be with me—in bed, thanks a lot—the night our female assassins' dorm caught fire.

Fake relationship or not, it had felt real enough when he broke it off.

"I am very pleased to meet you," Larissa says.

Her voice is sweet and she smiles at me. It's not a typical 'let me show you my fangs' vampire smile, but a real one. Like she actually is pleased to meet me. I didn't know nice vampires were a thing. She doesn't share the punk style of the vamps on campus either, judging from her cute little garden dress with a gossamer layover.

If she hadn't shown up with Val, I think this girl and I would be friends, instead of bitter rivals. I give myself a little mental shake. This girl is not my enemy. We are not going to roll around in the mud and pull each other's hair as we fight over a boy.

And yet, I can't stop my eyes from drifting over to the boy in question.

Larissa is way overdressed compared to Val. I want him to look visibly unhappy. But he's as unreadable as ever. I check out his snarky T-shirt for some sort of hint as to what's going on inside his head, but all it says is, *Give Blood. Give Life.*

"Pleased to meet you," I finally say in response to Larissa.

"Edie's my roommate," Tina informs her. "She's a shifter."

"Oh?" Larissa's eyes light up. "How interesting! I have always wanted to meet shifter."

"How about that?" Tina smiles at me, fangs glinting. "As the two newest students on campus, I bet you and Larissa are gonna be good friends."

Val finally speaks. "Edie, it looks like your group is getting impatient." He jerks his head in the direction of my team, who have all been avidly watching this entire interaction.

What does it say for my leadership abilities that I'd entirely forgotten about them?

"Right," I say lamely.

Tina flashes me a phony smile. "See ya later Edie...and you'd better have fed Vee while I was gone. If she has one limp leaf, you're dead."

Vee is Tina's pet Venus Fly Trap. She's bizarrely attached to the thing so she isn't joking about killing me. I actually did feed it. I have the bite mark on my finger to prove it.

"We must meet more later," Larissa says in her charming accented voice, again sounding totally sincere and non-sarcastic. She waves as Val turns without another word or glance my way.

I watch them walk away, hand in hand, Larissa excitedly pointing at this and that as they go. It's a relief when they turn a corner and disappear from view.

"Ouch. That was painful," Hermes says.

"I guess this means there's no chance of you getting back with Val," Greg adds, hopefully.

"If you're looking for a rebound, I'm around," Jordan winks. "I like strong women."

Hepa's the only one who doesn't comment, but she shoots me a pitying look, which is almost worse.

"Let's just go," I say, hurrying along in the direction that Hermes was leading us before I got vampire detoured.

Past the dorms but before the archives building is a little garden surrounded by pillars, nine in all, with a fountain at its center. The stone figure is of Hermes himself, stylized midflight, his winged feet dancing on the water's surface.

He is also completely naked.

I sigh. There's just no escaping Hermes' penis.

He goes to the fountain and the pillars light up. Two of them grow brighter than the others, a sheet of light appearing before them.

"That's the portal to our Grecian doorway." Hermes says.

"We can't get you all the way to where you need to be, but we can get you close."

"Don't worry," Greg says, pointing to the pack slung over his shoulder. "I brought the map you gave us last night."

I swallow. "And we get back how?"

Hepa groans. "Oh gods, don't you know anything?"

Hermes hands me one of the keys. "Throw it in the fountain on the other side. It's set it to let five pass through in case you find your mom."

"Great. Thanks." I take it from him. "And it's *when* we find my mom."

"That's the plucky attitude I like," Hermes says condescendingly.

"Wait," Hepa says. "We can't go wandering around Greece in our school uniforms." She has us stand in a circle and recites an incantation. Our uniforms change to normal clothes, khakis and light-colored tops.

"Oh yeah, um, good thinking," I say, embarrassed that I didn't think of it first.

"Unless you have further accessorizing to do, I suggest, you know...leave," Hermes tells us.

"Okay, let's go." I adjust my pack on my shoulders, hold my head high, and walk through the doorway.

Icy cold stings every bit of my body. I am in the midst of—

Nothing.

I'm either in the middle of the portal...or a walk-in freezer.

I force myself to take another step and the nothingness gives way to the sands of an endless desert. There are pillars and the fountain, with Hermes' stone penis staring me in the face, just like back at the Academy. But beyond that miles and miles of smooth silt.

One by one my team arrives behind me.

"What the..." Hepa says with a shiver.

"Is this Greece?" Greg asks.

"Does Greece have a desert?" I ask, feeling stupid.

Hepa says *no* at the same time Jordan says *maybe*.

"Greg, can you take a look around?" I ask, motioning to the sky.

"I mean, I could fly up there," he tells me, "but my vision is terrible during the day and that sun is brutal."

"We should just go back," Hepa says. "Obviously something has gone wrong."

Not the worst suggestion. Clearly Hermes was too busy staring at Jordan's abs to bother checking that our destination was correct.

I hesitate, not sure what to do. If we're in the right place, I'll seem like an idiot if we return without even looking around first. Also...I would like to defrost a bit more before immediately tucking our tails between our legs and retreating.

"Let's just check it out," I say.

Hepa is mid-scoff when the earth moves beneath us. I fall on my butt in the sand. Hepa's down with me, but Greg has turned into a bat and is hovering while Jordan gracefully maintains his feet.

"Earthquake," Hepa shouts, but then something pushes its way out of the sand.

It's a white tail with a nasty looking stinger at the tip that's at least the size of my arm. How big is the rest of the creature?

"Oh gods, no," I moan.

It's not an earthquake.

It's a monster attack.

The earth around us groans as a giant pale claw appears, then another. As the monster's head and beady eyes emerge, sand flows off its carapace like water.

My shivers are no longer from being cold as I take in the giant white scorpion standing before us.

His stinger slams into the earth, nearly impaling Hepa. Luckily, Jordan has already shifted into his panther form. He head-butts the scorpion, knocking it off-balance.

"Run," he growls at us. Only shifters can understand other shifters when they're in their animal forms, but Hepa doesn't need a translator—she's already running.

I scramble to my feet, ready to follow her lead, when it occurs to me—oh yeah, I don't have to be weak helpless little Edie.

I can be a dragon.

I'd bet my wings that dragon beats scorpion.

"Get out of the way," I shout to everyone.

Jordan switches back to human form and bounds across

the unstable earth scooping Hepa up in his arms. He runs with her while Greg, in his bat form, follows.

I face the scorpion head on, allowing my dragon side to take over. Since the Spring Fling, I've shifted a few times, and the feeling never changes. My wings sprout first, emerging from my back in a rush of red. They can change colors according to my mood but when I'm fighting, they're the color of blood. My spine arches, each vertebra elongating and sharpening, erupting from my back as spikes. Scales shimmer down my arms and legs. Fire chokes my throat.

Gods, it feels amazing. I. Am. A. Dragon.

And I am going to tear apart this monster that dared to come after my team.

I let loose a mighty dragon roar and the scorpion pauses a second before trying to sting me with its tail, darting the sharp dripping needle closer and closer. I let loose a blast of skin melting, body crisping, bad ass dragon fire.

The flame does absolutely nothing to the scorpion.

Oh crap. It must be fire resistant. I've done no combat training while in my dragon form. I slash with my claws but the scorpion easily dances back out of my reach.

I panic, flapping my wings. That at least gets the air moving, blasting the monster back a bit. When I'm airborne I spot Greg, hovering above Jordan, who is still carrying Hepa in his arms as he runs. It doesn't seem to be slowing Jordan down a bit. But he'll tire eventually. And the scorpion—

Is still in pursuit, gaining on them.

I swoop down toward my team, grabbing Jordan and Hepa in my claws and carrying them into the air. Greg follows.

I try to ignore Hepa cursing my leadership skills, but at

least they're out of the way of the scorpion and its giant deadly stinger. I circle and in the distance spot an area with some palm trees.

An oasis! Maybe the monster won't be able to track us that far away?

I give the scorpion a final look and notice it's stopped at a point, not moving forward. I go lower to get a better look and Hepa once again curses my name. What is the creature doing? Every time it tries to move past that point, a wall of air shimmers and sparks. Interesting.

I turn to the oasis and fly us there, dropping Hepa and Jordan onto some soft brush. Jordan easily lands on his feet while Hepa rolls a couple of times and gets to her knees, coughing up dirt.

I shift back into my human form. "Is everyone okay?"

"Just great," Hepa says, sarcasm dripping from every word. She spits out another mouthful of sand.

"What was that?" Greg squeaks, landing on my shoulder.

"That was a really big ass scorpion," Jordan, master of the obvious, adds.

"Can you shift back to human, Greg, so I'm not missing part of the conversation?" Hepa asks.

Chagrined, Greg shifts. And then all eyes are on me.

"So what are we going to do?" Greg asks.

"I don't know," I admit.

"Let's...catch our breath and regroup," Hepa says, getting to her feet. "By the looks of it, that scorpion was tasked with guarding that portal. It couldn't cross that magical barrier so it has to stay in a certain predetermined location, which is good because that means we're safe here. Bad because it means we're stuck."

"What if that thing has friends around?" Greg asks.

"Scorpions hate water and wet sand. If they come too near they could drown," Hepa says. "Didn't you guys take Monsters 101?"

"I must have missed that day," I mumble.

I take a deep breath, shivering. Our shadows are getting longer and the air is cooler.

"How is the sun setting?" Greg asks. "It's morning."

"Not here. Wherever here is," I say. "Sounds like we're safe for now. In the morning I'll fly us back to the fountain and the portals."

"And the scorpion," Hepa adds. "You'll fly us back to the scorpion. Good plan."

"Maybe we can get up early and sneak past it when it's sleeping," I suggest, even though I know it's a totally lame plan.

"Do scorpions sleep?" Jordan asks, and Hepa nods.

"They're nocturnal, but again, this one has been given a task," she adds. "It will fight to the death."

"Then we'll fight back," I say.

Greg paces nervously. I can tell he wants to change back to bat form. When adrenaline is running high like it is now, it's a struggle to not shift. "Why are we here and not Greece?"

"I'm gonna find out," I promise. "But first, let's get back to the Academy alive."

———

Later, Jordan decides to take a moonlit skinny dip and Hepa is at the edge of the water creeping on him. She was subtle at first but now is openly staring.

I mean, I am a bit too. It's hard not to. Jordan has an animal magnetism that draws you to him, and his penis is definitely something that whoever carved Hermes' statue might want to take a look at.

I adjust my gaze, feeling like a perv. Greg sits under a palm tree next to me.

"Gonna take a dip too?" I ask.

"Nah. Reminds me of Darcy too much. I'd rather not think about him right now."

"There's nothing wrong with remembering those who died."

I've lost so many people. My dad. My grandma. Even Ocypete...yeah, maybe it's better not to think about that right now. Too complicated.

"Well, I'm going in!" I say, stripping down to my underwear. The desert night air is cool but the water is still warm. I splash into the reservoir and float on my back. Just like Darcy taught me.

"If you don't mind me paying you a compliment..." Jordan says from a few feet away.

I could use a compliment about now. "Go ahead."

"You have a smokin' hot bod."

I stand and look at him, my feet touching the bottom. I can't help the shiver I feel. "Thank you, Jordan. You're not so bad yourself."

He gazes at me with his amber panther eyes, and I regret my decision to join him. I'd run away from Greg because I didn't want to talk about Darcy, or think about the dead. But being near Jordan makes me think other thoughts... thoughts that bring up memories of Val.

I flee the water. I don't need a complication.

We make a fire, or, Hepa does, casting a quick incantation with a tap of her finger. Then we eat a little of the food in our packs, Greg still wondering aloud how we ended up in the middle of...wherever we are.

I remember Ocypete, standing in front of me to shield a chimera from my blazing wrath, begging me to *THINK!!*

Ocypete had tried to turn me over to the monsters' side before the night of the attack. She'd convinced a few other students to spy for her, but the gods got wise and she had to kill her recruits so they wouldn't talk.

I think Fern might've been one of them. We haven't yet had a proper talk about that. Fern doesn't even know that I talked with Ocypete and she'd called Fern "one of hers." I just can't imagine Fern doing anything to hurt people. She's a healer!

But what if I'm wrong? What if she had a part in getting us sent to the wrong portal? Maybe the reason she didn't want to go on this mission had nothing to do with her girl-friend not liking it.

I hate suspecting a friend, but someone purposely sent us here...or at least, didn't want us to get my mom. I don't know where the portal keys are kept or who has access to them, but it's definitely something I have to find out when I get back to Mount Olympus Academy...if I get back.

Whoever did this sent us to a portal protected by a monster. They might have wanted to keep me apart from my mom—forever.

My heart pounds with all the questions. It seems like the more I learn about my past, the less I understand.

Or am I just being paranoid? Hermes might be a god, but nobody ever claimed he was a genius. It's not beyond him to completely mess up and grab the wrong key. Maybe he was just distracted by Jordan's midsection, and tossed the wrong one through the portal.

It is a distraction. A nice one too. He'd peeled off his shirt once Hepa got the fire started, then, like a true cat, got dangerously close to the source of warmth.

Soon, Hepa calls it a night. The rest of us are still too keyed up from the day, so we kick around ideas for tomorrow. But as it gets late and we get punchy, we start to become ridiculous. Jordan suggests we eat the notoriously disgusting beef chili meal pack.

"Give it a few hours," he says, "And we can kill that big bad scorpion with fart power."

Greg, not to be outdone, suggests we just invite the scorpion to join our side and attend MOA with us.

This cracks us up.

"Oh my gods!" I laugh. "Can you imagine Mr. Zee's face? Or Themis'?"

"Yeah, but Hermes would totally hit on him," Jordan adds.

When our laughter finally dies down, Greg yawns hugely and soon after shuffles off to bed. Jordan follows a little bit later. But I stay by the dying fire. I need to come up with a plan better than fart power.

Something crackles to my left, I spin around, my wings springing out as I prepare to shift. Then I spot Jordan up in one of the trees, watching the sands.

I sigh in relief and my wings relax, disappearing back beneath my skin. Slipping out from under my blanket, I go to the bottom of the tree.

"Can't sleep?" I ask.

He's down in a second, landing in the sand in front of me without a sound. His ninja skills are alarmingly hot.

"This is what I do," he says. "I watch. I can go days without sleep." He licks his lips and I can't help but follow the movement. "It's all about stamina."

I swallow and resist the urge to ask any follow up questions about Jordan's...stamina. "Any movement from our friend the scorpion?"

"Not that I can see, and I would see. I have excellent night vision."

Those eyes are on me again. This time I don't look away. I take a step closer. Why the hell not?

Jordan is game.

Val has a fiancée and has clearly moved on. Whatever was between us—if there was anything—is over. And I need to get over it before I seriously embarrass myself.

I lean in and kiss Jordan's smooth lips

He purrs into my mouth as his tongue invades. It rasps against mine, rough like a cat's.

I should've been expecting that, but I wasn't and I'm a little weirded out. I push that aside, focusing instead on the way he cups the back of my head in one oversized hand.

He adjusts me expertly, finding the perfect angle to deepen the kiss. I sink into sensation. Enjoying his hot mouth. His warm hard body. And his whiskers gently tickling my face.

Whiskers!?! What the what?!

I jerk back.

Yeah. I am definitely kissing a dude with cat whiskers.

I'm out.

I clear my throat. "Ugh, we probably shouldn't do this. I'm your team leader and if I make out with you, then I should probably make out with everyone."

"Yeah!" Jordan grins. "Team building orgy. I like it."

"No, no. Definitely—just no." I shake my head to make sure he gets it, "I think it's best if we keep our team non-orgiastic."

Jordan visibly deflates, but then after a moment shrugs. "You're the boss." He gives me a quick peck on the cheek and then springs back up into his tree.

His sweetness melts my heart but not enough to try

making out with a cat-man again. I think Jordan and I are meant to be strictly platonic.

I settle back beside the last dregs of the fire and even though I fight against it, my eyes eventually drift closed and I fall asleep.

7

Okay, maybe making out with one of my teammates in the middle of a crisis was a bad idea. We weren't as discreet as I thought either because everyone is acting weird. Hepa won't speak to me this morning, and Greg is answering all my questions in monosyllables.

On top of that, I woke up to Jordan happily peeing into the reservoir, not bothering to cover up, and apparently not realizing that he was contaminating our only water source.

Hepa and Greg reluctantly refilled their flasks from the farther end of the pool, with Jordan on their heels, apologizing sheepishly.

"Urine is water soluble," I tell them. "I learned that in non-magical school."

Hepa gives me the look of death while Greg mumbles something about me making excuses for my new boy toy.

Get it together, Edie, I think to myself.

I'm the leader. I'm the one who has to get us out of this. I went through those portals thinking *I'm coming, Mom*, then ended up doing everything wrong. I've got to get my game face on, or Mr. Zee and Themis won't ever let me off campus again—which means leaving Mom, Cassie, and maybe even Mavis out to dry.

Mavis would know what to do, I think, brushing away a tear. Back home in Florida she'd hadn't even blinked when a creepy crawly was in our bedroom. Instead she'd smashed it with a thick book. As official bug killer Mavis always flushed them down the toilet to get rid of them...

And Hepa said that scorpions can drown.

"Hey guys, I've got an idea," I call out, excited to be able to say that at last.

Greg and Hepa might be pissed at me, but I'm still the leader, and they snap to attention.

"We need to get to the portal, and back to campus," I say, to which Hepa rolls her eyes.

"Duh," she says. "But you may recall there's a giant scorpion in the way."

"Greg," I ask, ignoring her. "How strong do you think I am?"

"Huh?" he asks. "Um...like...really strong. You have opinions and aren't afraid to tell everyone what to do. But not so much that it's a turn off."

"Dude, it's never a turn off," Jordan says, with a wink.

I close my eyes. "Can we focus? I mean *physically* strong. In dragon form."

"Oh," Greg says, suddenly analytical. "Your wingspan is impressive, and you carried both Jordan and Hepa here without any trouble. So, you're definitely strong, but I don't know that it's ever been put to the test."

"It hasn't," I agree.

"Well, no time like the present," Hepa says. "And you've obviously got some sort of plan, so stop beating around the bush and just tell us already."

"Beating around the bush," Jordan softly snickers. We all stare at him. With a chuckle, he starts to explain, "Sorry, just thinking about beating around your bushes and..." He finally takes in our unamused expressions and his smile fades. "Right, right. Serious planning time. My bad. Go ahead, leader lady, give us the goods."

I frown at Jordan, really wishing I hadn't made out with him last night.

"I'm going to pick up that giant scorpion," I tell them. "But I'm going to have to be quick—and hold its tail in one claw so it can't sting me and its claws in the other so it can't snip me."

"And then?" Hepa asks. "If you drop it, it will just scramble back to us. Even from high up, I doubt it will do much damage."

"Not if I drop it in the water," I say. "And even if doesn't drown, you'll have time to make it through the portal, and I'll be right behind you. If the scorpion doesn't kill me."

"You're going to do this for us?" Hepa asks, something new in her look. Is it...respect?

"Edie, no—" Greg starts to say.

"Look," I cut him off. "I'm the team leader and this is my responsibility. Now listen up. Here's the plan."

I draw in the sand, my team circling around me. A little bit of confidence seeps into my voice.

"He'll see me coming, so he'll be looking for the rest of you. Greg, you're able to fly out of his reach, so you're safe enough. Jordan, you're fast as hell in panther form so I know you can outrun the scorpion."

Which leaves Hepa, our healer.

"Hey, I got a thought," Jordan says, sounding faintly surprised by this. He turns to Hepa. "Wanna ride me, babe?"

"Yes," she says emphatically, no hesitation in her voice.

"Wait," I interject. "Won't that slow you down? Or tire you out faster?"

Jordan shakes his head. "I told ya last night. This panther's got mad stamina."

Greg makes a disgusted noise in the back of his throat.

"Are you okay with, er, riding Jordan?" I ask her.

She folds her arms over her chest. "Yes. I just want to get out of here alive."

Okay then. I put my hands on my hips, hoping it looks authoritative. "Sounds like we have a plan."

8

Below me, my team is weaving through the sand, Greg flitting above the sleekly moving Jordan, a very happy Hepa on his back. The sun is rising behind us, which is to our advantage. Even if the scorpion is on alert for us, he's still a nocturnal creature, so the sunlight is our friend.

The pillars loom on the horizon, and sure enough, Hepa must have been right about the scorpion being tasked to guard them. It rises out of the sand, a replay of yesterday.

But this time, I won't make the mistake of trying to fry it.

It spots my team and dodges, taking a stab with its vicious tail. Jordan lunges one way, then the next, Hepa curled tightly to his back, her face buried between his shoulder blades. The scorpion is fast, but the cat is faster—and he has claws of his own. Jordan gets a decent swipe in but loses his balance due to the extra weight of a healer on his back. The cat rolls, and Hepa is knocked loose.

Greg dives at the scorpion's eyes, a mad dash that only infuriates the monster. But just like a house fly that won't stop hovering, it's the small things that matter.

The scorpion can't ignore Greg as he dips and dives, buzzing around the little hairs on its body.

Hepa explained it uses these to "see" so Greg messing with them makes the scorpion think there are more of us. It snaps at Greg and for a moment my heart leaps into my throat, but Greg flutters away.

Hepa gets to her feet, and Jordan—in human form now —grabs her hand. They dash toward the pillars together, kicking up sand. I see Hepa reach into her kit for the key, throwing it between the pillars. They light up, and two of my team disappear into the blaze.

"Get out of the way, Greg!" I cry, going in for the grab.

My friend zips out of danger, diving into the light of the pillars. His exit grabs the scorpion's attention and brings its focus straight up—to me.

I grab its tail, the stinger safely immobilized, but dripping glistening poison. I missed grabbing its claws so I'm dragging a struggling giant scorpion by its tail through the air. It folds its body up, snapping at me. Pain shoots through my forearm, but I don't drop it.

Instead the next time it lunges I reach in and get one of its pinchers in my other claw. Every muscle in my body struggles, flying with the extra weight, holding on to a mad scorpion, trying to avoid attacks.

I fear I'm about to drop it when we hit the magic barrier and pass through a wall of electricity. I'm fine, but the scorpion convulses and goes limp. It smells...toasty. I don't know if it's dead, but I'm not going to take any chances.

I fly directly over the oasis and drop it in the reservoir. Water splashes me, but I don't mind. It feels fantastic on my back and when I open my mouth, it sizzles on my tongue.

I hover over the area, waiting for the scorpion to emerge, but there's nothing.

I do a lot of gliding on the way back to the portal, too tired to pump my wings. Every part of me hurts and I'm bleeding. But I don't care. I just killed a giant scorpion—and I didn't use fire.

I used my head. I saved my team. I was a leader.

I land in the sand, going to back to human form and doing a little victory dance.

"Oh yeah," I say, shaking my butt. "Who drowned your creepy nightmare lobster ass? Edie did, you dumbass sand spider! What's my name, bitch?" I ask, cupping my hand to my ear.

"Edie! It's an old lady's name but this lady's got—" I fall silent.

Why isn't Greg saying anything?

He must have gone through without me.

Well, good. That was the plan.

In the silence I am suddenly very aware that the light no longer shines from the pillars around the fountain.

"Oh crap," I say aloud.

The portal is closed.

9

I walk over to where it had been, hoping the light will reappear. But it's just me and Hermes' penis. And miles and miles of desert sand.

Okay. I am lost in an unknown place. I am so tired I'm not even sure I could shift into dragon form, much less fly anywhere. And where would I go? Not back to the oasis, not with that scorpion possibly ready for round two. I mean, it's probably dead, but in every horror movie ever the creature comes back for one last stab just when the hero thinks everything is good.

I walk around the columns, then the fountain, then I actually get *in* the fountain. I have no idea how it works with the keys, much less how to open the portals without a key.

Okay, Edie, let's be smart about this. My team made it back. They'll send someone to get me. I just need to wait here.

The wind grows stronger, whistling past my ears and sending sand into all my orifices. I pull my shirt up so it covers my mouth and nose, but it's no use. It seems my luck is officially the worst, because if I'm not mistaken—this is a sandstorm.

I curse hotly. Too hotly. My breath blows a fiery hole through my shirt.

It's so awful, I can't help but laugh as I hunker further down into the fountain.

If I stay here, will I get buried alive? Is someone going to check on their pet scorpion and find me? Where the hell is the cavalry ready to save me?

Through the violent wind I swear I hear a voice. I can't make it out, but it sounds like...howling?

Maybe they sent a werewolf to find me!

I stand and feel my way out of the fountain, stumbling forward, the sand slippery beneath my feet. One foot in front of the other, I can only hope I'll walk into my rescuer.

I throw my wings out, deciding to risk flying, despite my exhaustion. Immediately the wind grabs them, the same way it would an umbrella on a stormy day. It pushes me back and then as I lift up, straight forward. I see the outline of a figure, weaving through the storm.

I squint and flap closer.

Whoever it is, they look worse off than I do. Wounded. Hurt. Maybe dying.

What if it's *not* my rescue squad but some random monster?

The figure crashes to the sand and I make a split-second decision to help them. Friend or foe, they're the one that looks like they need rescuing. I descend, the wind too much for my wings, and shield my eyes from the blowing sand. Only a few steps away from the fountain, I stumble onto the unfortunate creature.

I reach out, my fingers meeting fur. I'm beat, exhausted, and injured, but with a mighty wrench, I drag him back to the fountain, shielding us both with my wings, since the wind is at our backs now.

Exhausted, I climb into the fountain and lay down under the lip, hoping it will shield us both, for now.

———

The howling wind eventually lulls me to sleep, and when I wake up the sandstorm is over. I climb out of the fountain, shaking sand out of my hair. Not that it does much good. I'm pretty sure I have sand in every crack and crevice.

My stomach growls and I realize it's night, again. I haven't eaten and only slept in fitful sand drenched spurts. That kind of uneven sleep always leads to the trippiest dreams. Like I dreamt I saved a werewolf from the sandstorm.

I am shaking my head at this thought, when my dragon-sense tingles. The dragon-sense thing—and learning when to listen to it—is still new. But right now, it's clear: something is watching me.

I turn back toward the fountain. A glowing yellow eye stares back at me.

I gasp as a growling wolf stalks out of the fountain. It's mangy and dirty and missing one eye. It shakes the sand from its fur and studies me with the good one it has left.

I consider shifting, but I am beyond exhausted. Instead I pull my pack around and extract a piece of beef jerky. I take a bite, then hold it out...palm up, the way my dad taught me when meeting a new dog.

"It's okay, boy," I say. "I'm not gonna hurt you. Are you hungry? Don't you want some yummy jerky? It's so much tastier than I am."

He tilts his head, studying me. Then sniffs the air between us. A deep snuffling inhale.

Suddenly there's a naked bleeding boy in front of me.

"I'm...Nico," he says, holding out one hand, while the other covers a deep gash in his side. Blood drips onto sand. His fur must have been soaking it up before he shifted.

"Edie," I reply, taking his hand. "Are you..." I stop before I can ask if he's okay. He is so obviously not.

I watch as he shifts back into a wolf and then almost immediately slumps to the ground. His good eye flutters and I'm pretty sure he's gonna pass out. Maybe even die. I have no idea how much blood he's already lost.

As I rush to his side, my pack thumps against my back. I'm glad that like my uniform, it shifts with me. I'd almost ditched it for Operation Drown The Bug, but when I asked Hepa to carry it for me, she flat out refused.

"Survival 101," she'd said, with a disgusted head toss. "Your pack is your life."

At the time I thought it was a little overdramatic, but now...well, now I get it. Besides food and other basic necessities, I also threw in a can of instant healing stuff that I swiped from the infirmary a few months back. I used it pretty regularly during my flying lessons, so there's not a whole lot left. Reaching into my pack, I give the can a shake and hear the liquid slosh around. Yeah, there should be enough in there to at least close the wound.

Pulling the can out, I approach the wolf, er, Nico.

"Hey." I hold the can out. "I've got something here that might help you."

He shifts again and now I can see he's white as a sheet. "That's Academy stuff," he growls. "Are you from Mount Olympus Academy? My mom—" Before he can finish that thought his eyes roll back into his head and he passes out.

I hurry to his side, my finger on the spray button. But then I hesitate, wondering how he was going to finish that sentence. What if it was, "My mom says all Academy students must die?"

Should I use the last of my healing stuff on someone who might be my enemy?

The boy moans softly. He looks about my age. Maybe he is with the monsters—why else would he be out here? But he hasn't hurt me yet, or even tried to.

Dad used to say, "Assuming the worst of everyone around you is an ugly way to live." And I agree with him.

I spray Nico's side, using everything that's left in the can and then watch as his wound magically closes up. He doesn't look good as new, but I'm hoping it's enough so that he'll survive.

I also bind his head. The socket with his missing eye is pretty freaking gross. It's crusted with sand and blood. I wince and realize my own arm is cut—although the blood clotted a while ago. I give it a tentative look, but my shirt is firmly secured to the wound, caught up in the dried blood.

"We're a great pair," he says, making me jump. I hadn't realized he was awake. His voice is low and gravelly. "Do you have water?"

"Yes." I hold it to his lips, trickling a few drops in. There's not much left and with two of us drinking, it won't last long.

"Thank you," he breathes. "I thought I was a goner in that storm for sure."

"Why are you out here?" I ask, no longer holding out hope that he's part of my rescue mission. He looks starved and dehydrated and, honestly, like he's been lost in the desert for days—if not weeks.

"Are you from the Academy?" he asks instead of answering my questions.

I consider not answering but he continues, "'Cause it

would really suck to escape the monsters, just to be rescued by a monster sympathizer."

"I'm with the Academy," I assure him. "I was on a mission to rescue my mother from monsters, actually. It all went horribly wrong."

"Been there." He barks out a laugh that turns into a coughing fit.

"My team escaped through the portal but it closed on me. I'm waiting for help."

"Yeah, those things can be finicky...you have to all go through at once. If a gnat flies through it'll count as one of your team."

I want to ask him what he's doing out here. What happened to him. Who he is. But I see he's struggling to remain conscious.

"Just rest for now," I tell him. "I'm sure they'll come and get us really soon."

He looks up at me with his puppy dog eye and tells me, "I never thought I'd see anyone from the Academy again. I never thought I'd escape. You're beautiful." And passes out.

I'm left in the desert with a half-dead werewolf and a portal that won't open. But at least I can rock the crazy survivor lady look.

I smile at the thought because otherwise I'd cry.

10

N ight gives way to morning too soon and the sun rises over us, making the air shimmer with heat. Our last bit of water disappears too quickly. I've passed out on top of Nico when I notice the pillars light up. Through the portal steps—

I blink, certain I'm hallucinating.

"Val?"

He is followed by a team of people. Fern is with them. She runs to me.

"Edie, oh my gods. Let me look at you. We'll get you patched up, then back to the Academy to heal."

"Fern, help him," I motion to Nico. "He's in even worse shape."

"Who is that?" Val asks, as he unscrews a bottle of water and holds it my mouth. I gulp greedily and Val pulls it away. "Not too fast."

"He's from the Academy," I answer his question, my voice hoarse. Even with that sip of water, I feel like I've been gargling with sand for the past two days and honestly, I pretty much have been.

Val pauses. "Is that...Nico?"

What? Val knows him...of course. I keep forgetting that everyone else has been in school together for years. "Yes, that's his name," I say.

Fern exchanges a look with him. "He's been missing for almost a year—we thought he was dead. How did you find him?"

I shrug. "He found me."

"Okay, let's get you back." Val scoops me up in his arms and carries me to the gateway.

"More water," I whisper. "I'm thirsty...and...hot."

I close my eyes against the sun. I'm exhausted, so worn out that I can't even enjoy the feeling of Val holding me.

A soft rain starts to fall. Wetting my face. I lick my lips and I could swear the water tastes sweet.

"Better?" Val asks.

A soft sigh escapes me. It's the only response I can give as my head slumps against his chest.

This time when the cold nothingness takes me, I let it.

———

I regain consciousness in the infirmary, surrounded by people.

"She's awake!" Greg shouts.

"We can see that," Hepa says.

"Guys, keep it down," Fern warns. "You're not even supposed to be in here."

"Edie," Val leans in.

His cheeks are pink, like a little boy who's been playing out in the snow. Except it doesn't snow here and the pink only means that Val recently ate. It should be a turnoff knowing that he recently slurped down a rat blood smoothie. Yet somehow it isn't. The problem is...

"You're just so damn pretty," I say.

Val mouth curls into one of his rare smiles. He's wearing a shirt with a picture of a snake that says, *danger noodle*. I smile.

Then he says, "That's my girl." Those words burst the little bubble that had been forming between us.

"I'm not your girl."

I scooch up. My skin is raw and my arm is bandaged and sore, but I feel...not like death. Which is a start.

"And what the hell took you all so long to come back for me?" I try to shout, but it comes out more like a whisper.

"We tried." Greg looks near tears. "As soon as we got back and realized it had closed with you on the other side, we went to Hermes and Themis. But someone had been spelling the portal keys incorrectly—and not just the one we used. All of them were a mess! We just had to keep sending people through portals and bringing them back, and having them tell us where they'd gone... nothing was right, everything was mislabeled!"

Fern leans in. "Val was one of the volunteers; he just kept traveling and traveling. Portals are magic. And with magic, there's always risk involved. But Val wouldn't hear it. He kept going."

"And Fern was at my side the entire time," Val inserts quietly. He's moved to the other side of the room—near the door like he can't wait to leave. "She insisted."

"Because I should have been with you to begin with!" Fern bursts out, tears filling her eyes. "Marguerite was trying to protect me by asking me to stay behind, but I should have been there with you. This is all my fault!" Her usually calm face spasms as she bursts into tears. She covers her face with her hands.

"It's not your fault," Greg says, resting a hand on Fern's shoulder. "Whoever messed with the keys is to blame. And whoever it was, is a traitor."

Fern isn't comforted. Another sob escapes her, and her whole body shakes.

"Well, it all worked out," I say. "I mean, I wouldn't have found Nico, otherwise."

But I'm not thinking about the werewolf boy. I'm thinking about Val, and trying not to meet his gaze. I wonder how Larissa felt about her fiancée insisting on leading the rescue mission to find me.

"I owed you one after you saved me at the Spring Fling. Guess we're even now," he tells me, then walks away, no sign of emotion on his face. No flicker of what I saw when he emerged through the portal.

I sigh.

"I believe Ms. Evans needs her rest," Themis' voice booms from behind everyone. "I asked you all to leave her in peace."

"How's Nico?" I ask before they're sent away.

"He's resting, as you should be," Themis says.

"Oh my gods, Edie," Fern says. "I can't believe you brought him back. Everyone thought he was dead."

"Yeah," Greg says. "You're a hero...again."

"Of course she's a hero. She saved all our butts," Jordan tells them. "And we have nice butts."

"Yeah, you did good," Hepa tells me with a tight smile.

"Enough," Themis says. "Go. Now."

She shoos them away, repeating that I need my rest. But I'm not fooled. Themis came here to talk to me, and she wants me alone.

That's fine by me, as I've got my own questions.

"Edie," Themis says, sitting on the side of my bed. "You're not the result of a bat and ostrich shifter mating."

Okay, so that was my first question. Now, I've got another one.

"Then why would you say that?" I yell as loud as my parched throat will allow. She *shushes* me with a motion, glancing around. She mutters something under her breath. It feels like the air around us gets heavier, and everything further than three feet away is blurry, like we're at the center of a snow globe.

"Is that a cone of silence spell?" I ask her. "When do I get to learn the cool stuff?"

"You're not a magic student," she reminds me. "You're on the assassin track. And as to why I said you were a bat-ostrich hybrid, that's because having Mr. Zee interested in you is not in your own interests. Do you understand?"

I lick my lips. "Um... I'm trying, but—no."

"Mount Olympus Academy has certain rules about relationships between students and teachers."

"Um, yeah, any not-creepy place does."

"Yes, but, Edie, we're talking about *gods* and *goddesses*. We are not accustomed to being told what to do, and following rules does not come easily to us. Even rules we ourselves make."

I think about Hermes' wandering hands and Mr. Zee's jokes before we left. "So, there are rules, but you can't make the gods follow them?"

"For the most part, they do," Themis says. "Imagine our enrollment rate if parents of paranormal students knew that their children were being preyed upon?" She shakes her head. "No, even the gods know the students are more valuable as warriors than bedmates."

"But?" I ask, sensing her hesitation.

"But," she says warily. "There are still gods—and goddesses—who put their desires above the law."

I remember the Spring Fling, how Cassie had told me it was really just an excuse for Persephone to check out all the male students and pick out a boy toy for the next few months.

"And..." Themis clears her throat. "Mr. Zee's tastes have been known to be a bit... exotic."

"Right," I say, nodding. "He seemed really into the idea of banging my dragon mom."

Themis raises her eyebrows, urging me to continue.

"And..." I go on, watching her to see if I'm getting it right. "Since he's into a dragon mom, he'd also be into...the idea of...banging..." I can't say it, so I just point to myself.

Themis nods.

"EW!" I say. "That's gross!"

"Agreed."

I mean, Mr. Zee is definitely hot and all, but he's also ancient. Literally. I mean, just ew.

"Rarities are his specialty," Themis says. "And since you obviously are a dragon, I had to come up with a lie that would make you less attractive to him."

"So you said I was a bat-ostrich baby?" I ask. "How does that...?"

Then I remember how Mr. Zee had reacted, how upset he got about the mixing and diluting of blood.

"You told him I was—"

"A Moggy," Themis says.

"A what?"

"A Moggy. That's the impolite term for children of—"

"Never mind, I get it." Of course the gods have a mean name for those of mixed blood. "So, I'm not a *moggy* then?"

"Well..." Themis hesitates, which is weird. "It's hard to say for sure without knowing who your father was." She clears her throat and when she speaks again, her voice is crisp. "Regardless, it is best for Zee to believe so."

Mr. Zee's very clear hatred for the mixing and mingling of species—even two different kinds of shifters—was powerful. If he thought I was the result of that, he'd be turned off by me.

"You lied so that Mr. Zee won't try to bang me?"

"Yes, and it worked," Themis says. "However, I should inform you that Mr. Zee hasn't quite been well these last few hundred years. He's been around a long time and—"

"Right, I know. Merilee told me that gods and monsters aren't necessarily immune to things like dementia."

She'd been talking about my flying instructor, Ocypete, when she told me that. And maybe that was true. Maybe Ocypete had lost her mind in the end, trying to convince me to switch sides and leading an assault on the school we all call home.

"Yes, but in addition to being forgetful, Zee's impulse control has lessened," Themis adds. "Not that he was ever the epitome of control. But still, despite his memory problems he does sometimes get stuck on a certain idea. And having a dragon on campus seems to be one of them. He's asked Merilee to continue digging into the records. I don't think he's fully accepted our bat/ostrich hybrid story."

"Okay," I say, leaning back on the pillow, suddenly tired. "So that's bad, right? Should I start carrying a magical mace or something?"

"No, nothing like that," Themis assures me. "If he refuses to accept one lie, we simply come up with another. Eventually his interest will wane." She claps her hands suddenly and a slightly manic smile lights her face. "We could have quite some fun with it!"

"Sounds...so fun," I agree.

I slip off to sleep thinking Themis could probably use some time off.

11

W hen I wake again, I'm alone. Or I think so, until a familiar gravelly voice says, "You're finally up."

I sit up, the blood rushing to my head and making me feel woozy. I give myself a moment and then I spot him.

I no longer have the room to myself. Nico is now on the hospital bed next to mine. I prop myself up with some pillows while he gives me a toothy grin.

"Edie, the girl who saved my life."

He looks a lot better, with color in his cheeks and an eyepatch covering his ruined socket. He actually looks quite dashing, like a werewolf-pirate hybrid.

"I didn't realize you were such a celebrity around here. A dragon shifter?"

I blush. "It sounds cool, but I recently found out it probably just means I'm a Moggy. You know? Like some interspecies boot-knocking is in my past." I blush even harder. Who even says 'knocking boots?' I know Themis wanted me to spread the lie, but this is beyond embarrassing.

But Nico just shakes his head. "If you're the result of

interspecies mingling, I'm all for it," he says. Then with a slight frown, adds, "So long as you keep it in the shifter family."

Suddenly I'm highly aware of the fact that if he and I 'knocked boots' it would be 'keeping it in the family' and why am I even thinking about this?

Oh my gods, Edie, get a grip.

Nico frowns as he studies me even more intently. It's hard not to squirm beneath the intensity of his gaze. "You don't know who your parents are, then?"

"No." I look down and pick at the pilling on the blanket covering me. "I thought I did, but it turns out they weren't my real parents and they basically lied to me my whole life."

"Not your whole life. Seems they must've come clean if they're trying to find your birth parents now."

"Yeah, no." I clear my throat which has suddenly become thick. "My dad died and my mom was taken by the monsters. That's why I was out in the desert. I was leading a mission to find her, but the portal keys got all messed up."

Nico rubs a hand across his heavily-stubbled jaw. I can't help but compare him to Val. Everything about Val is liquid and smooth and cold. Nico on the other hand is rough and ragged...and hot.

He frowns. "That shouldn't happen."

"Yeah, I know." I hesitate, unsure how much I should confide in him. "I guess all the keys were actually wrong. It looks like someone messed with them on purpose." He still looks concerned, so trying to reassure him, I add, "Themis will get it figured out. If anyone can, it's her."

"Themis?" Nico sits up straighter. "She knows how to twist things so they suit her, convince you of things that aren't the truth. Mr. Zee trusts her too much and gives her too much leeway—" He stops himself. "I shouldn't be saying this. She was here, watching you while you slept. I thought it was weird, but I don't know, maybe you two have a thing."

"No! There's no thing. We're not a thing." I mean, I guess I trust Themis but I want to know what Nico has to say.

I swing my legs over the side of the bed and lean closer to Nico, not wanting to be overheard.

"She's who told me I might be a Moggy."

"Yeah, I snuck out of bed to stretch my legs when she was here. I noticed Themis was quick to put up a silence shield, but I don't need to hear what she said to know that if it comes out of Themis' mouth, it's not the truth. My mom and I have been saying for years now—she's gotta go. If she stopped getting in Mr. Zee's way and just let him run the Academy as he sees fit—"

"Well, I don't know about that..." I say, trying to find a diplomatic way to let Nico know I'm not exactly on team Zee either. Especially when Nico is clearly a superfan. His one good eye is lit up with a wolfish glow, and he doesn't even seem to hear me.

"You're obviously something special, Edie, and Themis doesn't like when people are too special. It was the same with my mother. She was kicked out for not falling into line, for refusing to bow and scrape for Themis."

Nico looks around, making sure no one else is nearby, before leaning in toward me. We are now both sitting at the edges of our beds, knees nearly touching. His breath fans my face.

"That's all gonna change soon. I just got a message from my mom. Mr. Zee's eyes were opened when monsters invaded that dance. It happened on Themis' watch. He finally realizes he needs to take more control. And he's starting with the summer semester special guest instructor.

Hermes booked old man Priapus, because he loves his sex-ed class. But Mr. Zee has a better idea."

Nico grins. I don't even know what he's talking about, but his enthusiasm is infectious. Also, anything that will get us out of sex-ed is okay in my book. Grabbing hold of my hands, he squeezes them tight. "This summer, we're learning real world survival skills with my mother, Maddox Tralano."

Nico looks at me expectantly. As if he just announced his mom was Kate Winslet or the Queen of England. I am clearly meant to be impressed.

"Um...wow," I say. "Your mom who got kicked out of the Academy is returning to teach."

"Yup. Themis is gonna lose her mind." He flashes me a toothy grin.

"Hello!" Fern bustles into the room. "Nice to see my two favorite patients getting along so well!"

Nico immediately withdraws, dropping my hands as the light in his eye goes out. "Yeah," he says, the one syllable flat and disinterested.

I'm surprised at this sudden change. He's being so rude to Fern. Which is weird because everyone loves Fern. It's an unwritten campus rule—be nice to Fern.

Catching my eye, Fern gives a little 'what can you do' shrug. Peeling up my bandage, she attempts to smooth over the awkward atmosphere. "So, I don't know if you heard, Edie, but we all thought Nico had died. He was out on a mission with another student—"

"The traitor," Nico growls.

Fern hesitates. "Yes, Emmie was a traitor. We didn't realize at the time."

"When I realized what she was, she tried to kill me." He laughs, bitterly, and suddenly I am seeing a whole different side of him. "She took my eye, but not my life," he scoffs. "She left me for dead. When I tried to make my way back to the Academy, the monsters caught me. They couldn't have been more pleased that I was alive. That way I was...useful."

I wince, aware what that must mean, and where all his other injuries must have come from.

"They didn't get anything out of me, though," he says, jaw tense. "It takes more than monsters to break a Tralano."

"Well, all's well that ends well," Fern chirps, but the smile she gives me is strained. I wonder if—like Cassie—she was friends with Emmie.

I never met her, but have heard her story many times. She was on a mission with another student—Nico, I guess. They were captured. Nico was killed...or not. And Emmie escaped, making it back to Mount Olympus Academy. They thought she was a hero, but then discovered she'd been turned by the monsters and was a traitor instead. Before she could be questioned, Emmie and her boyfriend, Derrick, escaped.

"All's well that ends well?" Nico sneers. "Easy for you to say, witch. You didn't spend almost a year being tortured in a monster prison cell."

Fern sighs.

"Nico is not a fan of non-shifters," she explains away his casual bigotry to me as she finishes securing a new bandage and turns toward Nico. "He hates vampires on principle and only tolerates us witches because occasionally he has need of a healer." And with that she rips off his bandage with a lot less care than she did mine.

Nico grunts. "Who could hate those gentle healer hands?"

Fern laughs and presses her hand to Nico's chest. "Lie back so I can check your eye socket."

He's surprisingly obedient. Only softly growling, "watch it," as she pours something that bubbles and hisses as it touches his skin.

"There you go," Fern says after replacing the bandage over Nico's eye. "You should be good as new by tomorrow. Not including the eye, of course."

She starts to walk away, and Nico grabs her hand. Surprised, and maybe a little scared, she spins.

Nico gives her one of his disarmingly charming canine smiles.

"Thank you." He says it softly, then releases her and leans back into his bed, looking the other way, almost as if he's embarrassed by his own decency.

Fern's smile is tight. "I guess this makes me your favorite witch."

"Nope," Nico quickly replies. "That's Cassie. She's the reason I got away. And once you tell me I'm healthy as I'm gonna get—I'm going back for her."

12

"What?"

Fern and I are both on his bed in an instant, and there's a small smile on Nico's face that tells me he doesn't mind the attention. But that's not my focus right now.

"A witch named Cassie?" I ask.

"I guess she's technically a seer."

Oh gods, it *is* Cassie. "Where?" I ask, impatiently.

"Where I was held," Nico says. "Out in that gods-forsaken desert. They brought her in a few weeks ago—"

"Did they hurt her?" My wings break out at the thought, blood red, and angry.

"Whoa." Nico's one good eyebrow flies up, and I have to turn my head to keep from frying him with a blast of fire from deep in my lungs that I can't control. If they did one-tenth of the things to Cassie that they did to Nico—

"No, no," he says, truly alarmed. "She's fine. They had big plans for her. Not a hair hurt."

"Edie," Fern says, eyeing Nico. "I think it might be best to have this conversation later. Nico's recovering and he's my patient—"

"No!" A last, bright burst of fire comes out with the word. "I want to know everything about Cassie, and I want to know it now."

Apparently being able to breathe fire isn't only for the circus; it's also totally useful for making your point. Despite Fern's frown, Nico tells me about waking up to find that the cell next to his was now occupied. Cassie had been scared and crying, but also worried about Nico and his wounds.

"She wanted to help me," Nico said. "Even though she was also locked up." Nico frowns. "She also kept calling the jail the Ritz Carlton and saying she thought it would be nicer. I guess one of the monsters made a joke and it went over her head."

"Yeah, that's definitely our Cassie," I say. "Then what happened?"

He quickly explains how he and Cassie hatched a plan to spring him loose. He wanted her to go, as well, but Cassie told him her best friend was coming to get her. She'd seen it in a vision. Also, she was pretty certain the monsters wouldn't hurt her.

"Because she's Merilee Madges' daughter," Nico adds. "She said her mother had created a spell that passes all of her knowledge of Mount Olympus Academy—the history, the secrets, everything—to her daughter upon her death. And the monsters wanted that."

"So, they'd never hurt Cassie," Fern reiterates, highlighting the positive. "They'd want her cooperative."

"No, but she's useless to them as long as Merilee is alive," I say, thinking. "She may be in danger. We don't know who sabotaged my mission but there's clearly a traitor on campus. Their next mission might be to kill Merilee."

"I..." Fern bites her lip, looking doubtful. But I don't need to convince her; as long as Themis believes me, Merilee will be safe and sound.

"Cassie helped you escape? How?" I ask Nico.

"She foresaw that one of the guards would..." Nico grimaces, disgust clear on his face. "Go into labor."

"Childbirth is a beautiful and natural thing," Fern says, her tone gently reprimanding.

"Not when it's a manticore," Nico snipes back. "Anyway, Cassie knew this manticore was gonna go into labor, and apparently she had some healing courses?"

He looks at us, a question on his face.

Fern nods. "A few. Cassie kind of...well, we never really knew where she would fit. I mean, she tried to be a healer but she accidentally stitched someone's hand to their leg and that was a whole thing—"

"Right, fine." Nico holds up his hand, like he's in charge of who talks when. And clearly right now—it's his turn. "Anyway, the other guard was trying to help the manticore and things were..." He grimaces again, then sees Fern's stern look. "Well, things were happening fast. Cassie offered up her healing skills, and they let her out. She lifted the keys from the guard and slipped them through my bars. I unlocked my cell, passed them back out, and she replaced them on the guard's belt. You know, I would see her around the Academy sometimes. I never paid much attention to her but...she saved my ass. She's a good friend to have."

"She really is," I agree, a knot in my throat.

"Then it was just a waiting game," he continues. "As soon as their backs were turned—it didn't take long, since a newborn manticore wail is very distracting—I slipped out."

"Into a sandstorm," I add. "Not exactly great timing."

"But I found you," Nico says, his fingers brushing mine. "I would argue it was perfect timing."

"Actually, *Edie* found *you*," Fern corrects, but neither one of us pay her much attention. My wings have slid into a deep purple, shimmering with my pulse.

"Could you locate the place where you were imprisoned again?" I pull my hand back, determined to focus.

"Absolutely," Nico nods. "The foul smell is unmistakable. It carries for miles."

I nod. "Then we're going. You and me, right now."

But Fern is shaking her head. "No way. First of all, Nico is in no way ready to leave campus again. Secondly, Themis will never approve another mission so soon after what happened last time."

"What happened last time is that I killed a giant scorpion," I say. "The mix-up with the portal wasn't my fault."

"Regardless, you both need to recover..."

"Don't you want Cassie back?" I interrupt, giving her a hard look.

"Of course," Fern says, tears in her eyes. "But am I supposed to just watch you go back into certain danger?"

"The other option is leaving *Cassie* in danger," I tell her. "And I'm not okay with it. Cassie was the first person I met here, the first friend I had. I'm not leaving her with monsters. I don't care if they aren't physically hurting her. This is her home; she's never even left the Academy before. She's probably terrified."

My voice breaks on the last word, as I realize how true it is.

"I'm going after her, and I'm going as soon as this werewolf can walk."

"I can walk," Nico says, and then adds with a dangerous smile, "And fight too."

"Oh my gods." Fern stands up. "Is there any way I can talk you out of this?"

At Fern's repeated protestations, a flicker of unease ripples my thoughts. Yeah, we're her patients and she's worried about our health, but maybe it's more than that.

Ocypete identified Fern as one of the traitors, and if it's true, then maybe she'd rather not have us foiling the monster's plans for Cassie.

After the battle at the Spring Fling dance, Mr. Zee told me that when Ocypete killed the students she'd recruited, her goal was to make it look like I—the only fire breather on campus—was the culprit. Her goal was to further alienate me from the student body, thus making me more susceptible to her offer to join the monsters.

I want to pull Fern aside and demand answers right now, but if I start to question Fern now, that means I'm gonna have to really figure out who was lying to me—Ocypete or Mr. Zee. But now is not the time.

Cassie needs me, and I'm going to her.

With a one-eyed werewolf in tow.

Fern throws her hands up. "Fine. If I can't talk you out of it, the least I can do is make sure you don't get killed."

She rummages in a cabinet, producing a vial.

"Drink this," she says to Nico. "It's a short-term energy burst. Maybe eight hours. It will mask your pain, but your adrenaline levels will be through the roof. You'll feel invincible but—please try and remember—you are not. Do you understand?"

Fern's voice is firm now, a nurse in charge. Nico nods, taking the vial. "You really aren't half bad, you know."

"Enough with the back-handed compliments," she tells him. "It's not as charming as you think."

She turns to me. "You'll want to put a fresh uniform on so you can spell it. The hospital gown won't shift with you."

Fern points to the cotton gown with little ties barely holding it together. I was so focused on Cassie, I totally forgot I was walking around in this thing. I don't even have underwear on!

Clutching the gown close, I grab the pile of clothes Fern offers and take them behind a curtained area to change.

"Nico, here's some clothes for you," I hear Fern say.

"Naw, I'm good," he answers. "I don't wear the uniform on missions. My mom taught me those types of things make us too reliant on spells and magic. Weakens our natural animal instincts."

"Uh-huh," Fern answers, clearly skeptical. "So, you're going to wear the pajama bottoms and a T-shirt you just pulled out of the lost and found bin?"

I come back out in time to see Nico shrug. He's wearing a Henley that's too tight...but definitely not in a bad way.

Fern shakes her head but doesn't argue any further. "I can get you the portal key you need. Hermes has a few of the witches he trusts doing the reclassification. It's a huge mess, and he's in a lot of trouble with Mr. Zee for letting this happen in the first place. If I tell him I can put in some over-time, I'll be able to slip in and get the key."

"Great," I say. "How about right now?"

Nico checks a pretend watch on his wrist. "Yeah, right now works for me."

Fern closes her eyes and sighs. "All right. No time like the present, I guess. Let's get Cassie back."

13

Nico and I make our way to the portal. Fern promised to meet us there with the portal key.

After that potion she gave him, Nico looks fine—you'd barely know he was injured. He walks with an agile gait, like he can spring into action at any moment.

She'd also warned that it would send his testosterone into overdrive, and it definitely has. He can't keep his eyes off my chest. He also keeps shifting back and forth. In wolf form he darts away and then bounds back after a few minutes. Once he shifts human again, he falls into step beside me, breathing hard with exertion.

I can't help but wonder if he's running off an erection.

We go the long way around the quad, to avoid any crowds of students.

Like my previous mission, this quickly fails as well.

We manage to smack right into Jordan, hanging with a few of his spy class friends. He glances up at us and I hope he'll just let us walk by, but no such luck. He excuses himself from the group and jogs over.

"I didn't know you were out," he tells us.

Nico plants himself in front of me, almost like he doesn't even want Jordan to look at me. I'm pretty sure it's the testosterone amping up his animal protective instincts. It's annoying, but as long as he doesn't pee on my leg to mark his territory I can deal with it.

I elbow my way past Nico as he finishes giving Jordan a long slow up and down look. "I feel like there's a lot you don't know," Nico sneers.

"Yeah." Jordan isn't even insulted. "That's why I ask questions." He turns to me. "I thought you were stuck in the infirmary."

Hepa appears out of nowhere. "They're supposed to be."

"Hey, Hepa!" Jordan grins. "Wow, this is like the tenth time we've accidentally bumped into each other today. Small campus, huh?" There isn't a trace of mockery in his voice. He's completely sincere.

I cut my eyes at Hepa as she simultaneously blushes and scowls. It might've escaped Jordan's notice, but them bumping into each other is no accident. Hepa is into him. Which is fine with me, but why did her stalking of Jordan have to be right now?

"So then, what's up?" Jordan asks all of us. "Were you looking for me?"

Nico growls a laugh. "Why would we be looking for you?" He starts to walk in the direction of the portal, but of course, Jordan and Hepa follow.

"You're going somewhere, aren't you?" Hepa asks.

"Yes, away from you," Nico informs them.

Jordan tilts his head. "Where are you really going, Edie?"

"Would you two please shut up," I whisper yell. "For a spy, you're very obvious!"

Jordan lowers his voice. "Well, wherever you're going, I'm coming. You guys are not exactly fighting fit."

"No," Nico tells him. "This is a two-person mission and..."

"Hey Greg," Jordan shouts over my shoulder. "Come join our secret mission."

I shake my head. Jordan's spy classes have obviously not yet covered "quiet voices."

"Secret mission?" Greg asks, from behind me. "What secret mission?"

I hang my head. "Look guys, Nico and I got this. We don't need you to come." We probably could use the help, but I just led these guys into danger, and they almost didn't get back out.

"This is a quick and dirty thing," Nico agrees.

"I like it quick and dirty," Jordan says. "I mean, I like it any way I can get it."

"Yes, he doe—" Hepa clears her throat. For a second she was looking at Jordan all googly-eyed, but now they snap back into focus. "Don't you need backup?"

"Yeah," Greg chimes in. "I mean, Nico is literally missing an eye. What if he needs to do something that involves depth perception?"

"I can see better with one eye than you can with both of yours, little bat," Nico barks.

"Okay, everyone, over here, now!" I say, motioning them to an empty bench. They gather around. "Look, this is off book," I tell them in a low voice. "The teachers don't know about it. We could get into some major trouble."

"Okay, I'm in." Jordan says.

"Really?" I ask. "Just like that?"

"Yeah, me too," Greg says.

Hepa also nods and gives me a 'why not' shrug.

"I didn't even tell you yet that the mission is to rescue Cassie..."

"Oh, it's for Cassie?" Greg says. "Then I'm double in!"

I shake my head. Gods, I love my friends.

I give Nico a look. "They want to help. And we probably will need them."

"Fine," he says in a low rumble. "Everyone needs to make their way over to the portal. *Discreetly*. If you're not there when we're ready to leave, you're not coming with us."

Everyone agrees and heads off in different directions, but first they break like we're a football team and it couldn't be more obvious, even if we did a cheer first.

"Amateurs," Nico grumbles.

I nudge him. "Are you always this grumpy or is it the potion from Fern?"

His one eye blinks at me in surprise. "Grumpy? Did I take a bite out of anyone?"

"Well, no. Not literally." I hesitate, not wanting to get in a fight before our mission. But at the same time, I feel like it needs to be said. "But you were super rude to my friends."

"Rude." Nico scoffs. "I was honest. That's the way my mother raised me. Mad Maddox doesn't take any shit. Anyway, this isn't charm school. And I'm not here to make friends. I'm training to be a warrior. If everybody had my focus, maybe we'd actually win this war and finish all those monsters off for good."

On that dark note we arrive at the portal. Hepa and Jordan show up a few minutes later. We wait quietly—with Nico's attitude it seems safer to avoid making conversation. Finally, Fern comes running toward us. After taking in that there are now four of us gathered by the portal, Fern takes out two keys. "Okay I'll have to adjust the spell, I thought it was just us going but it shouldn't be a problem to change the number..."

"What's going on?" Hermes asks. What is with my luck?

I try to act natural but honestly, we all look super shady.

"Hermes!" Fern says, shoving the keys into my hands. She takes his arm and steers him away. "I was just looking for you. I wanted to talk to you about sex."

"Really?" he asks, utterly enthralled. "I thought you worshipped at the altar of Lesbos? Are you perhaps curious about the other side of things?" The rest of us are forgotten, Fern's masterful redirection taking up all of Hermes' interest.

"Well, yes. The sex-ed class. I heard it was cancelled. That's really a shame..." She leads him off.

I let out a relieved breath. "I guess it's just us then..."

"Don't leave without me," Greg squeaks in bat form, landing on my shoulder. "I shifted because I wanted to be extra sneaky but I got side-tracked by a tasty insect so I thought I'd grab a snack, but now I'm here..."

Hepa shakes her head. "From all of that I understood 'leave', 'extra', and 'insect' so I'm a bit confused..."

"It's not important," Nico says. "We should go before we're caught."

"Yes," I agree. "Fern said this was the outgoing key... Hepa, can you spell it to let more people through?"

Hepa nods and takes the key. "Magic isn't a bottomless well," she tells us. "Using it tires witches out so I'll have to stay by the portal and rest while you go. That way I can heal Cassie if she needs it when you return, and I'll be sure to have enough power left to get us home."

"Sounds like a plan," I tell her. "And let's be sure we all go through the portal together this time. No one gets left behind."

"That wasn't our fault..." Greg says, shifting into human form. "Except maybe it was because I swear I was bitten by a mosquito or something, like maybe a mosquito hopped a ride with me through the portal and it would've counted as a living thing. One nasty mosquito, too," he says, reaching up to scratch between his shoulder blades. "You should see the bite. I swear it's infected because—"

"I'll take a look when we get back," Hepa says quickly, and right on time. Beside me, Nico was just starting to bristle.

Hepa throws in the key and the pillars light up. We go once again into the desert, but at least this time we know what we're facing. A monster stronghold.

At least I'm not facing it alone.

14

This time there's no scorpion watch dog. Still, I make sure that Hepa wants to stay behind.

"Are you sure?" I ask again. "We have no idea what else might be out here, or if they're patrolling for Nico. Remember, this is entirely unsanctioned, so no one is going to come looking for us, if—"

She smirks. "I'm pretty sure if you go missing again, Val will quickly volunteer to lead a search party. Are you *sure* the two of you are broken up?"

"Val?" Nico growls. Thick sideburns form on his face as he turns to me, getting right up in my face. "You dated a *vampire*?"

I plant my hands on his chest and shove. He doesn't move. Not an inch.

It's intimidating having an angry werewolf boy all hopped up on testosterone in my face.

But it's also pissing me off. I can feel my dragon firing up, ready to give Nico the extra crispy treatment.

"Hey man, I get it." Jordan slings an arm around Nico's shoulder, pulling him away from me. "It's like the world is this delicious babe buffet. But there's no sneeze-guard. So who knows who's been there first?"

Nico jerks away from Jordan, he breathes hard, his chest visibly rising and falling. But he doesn't come any closer to me.

Jordan, meanwhile, continues philosophizing. "The thing you gotta realize, man, is there's more than enough for everyone. So, who needs a sneeze-guard anyway, when it just makes it harder to reach the babes?"

"I get it. You're not at all picky about who you dine on," Nico says with a shake of his head.

Jordan frowns. "Not cool, dude. Don't slut shame me."

"Yeah, that's not cool," Greg says.

"Guys, can we please focus up," I ask. Nico shoots me an apologetic look. It's not an actual apology, but it's enough to make my dragon stand down.

Then two seconds later, it nearly bursts out of me again as Nico pivots from being a dick to being a total bossy-pants. I mean, I get it. He's way more experienced at this than I am, but he also was captured by monsters so...

"Panther," Nico says, and Jordan steps forward. "You're with me. We'll scout the area and report back. I think it's best if Edie creates a distraction while I extract Cassie."

"Hold on a second," I say. "Who put you in charge?"

Nico looks surprised. "Every team needs a leader. I've held that position many times and assumed—"

"I've been a team leader too," I cut in. "At this exact spot, actually."

"Yeah, man," Jordan chips in. "Edie's a great leader. And a great kisser. Two things I learned on our last mission."

"Jordan, please don't help," I mutter.

"I *knew* you made out with him," Hepa snaps.

"Unbelievable!" Greg adds. "First Val. Now this wolf guy

and in between you had Jordan. When are you gonna give me a chance?"

"I'm a person, not a pie, Greg. Everyone doesn't get a piece."

"You're not entitled to her affections," Jordan jumps in.

"I know, I know," Greg nods. "I'm just saying, I can do things with my tongue that these other guys probably can't—"

"Seriously?" Hepa rolls her eyes.

"Wait, I'm interested in hearing more," Jordan says. "Give us the deets on the tongue action."

I throw up my hands. "Fine, Greg, let's get it on. Right here in the sand. Is that really want you want?" I ask, sarcasm dripping from every word.

He tilts his head, thinking. "Is that on the table—like for real?"

Hepa laughs and Jordan starts to say something else when Nico barks, "ENOUGH!"

Amazingly, we all go quiet. He points to Greg.

"Bat shifter…"

"Greg," Greg tells him with a glare.

"Whatever. You're gonna be plan B, once we're inside. You're small enough to fit through the bars of Cassie's cell so if I'm detained you'll need to get the keys to her. Do you think you can handle that?"

"Yeah, I got it. I'm Plan B," he tells Nico with a sigh.

"Or," I interrupt, feeling bad for Greg. "Why don't we send him on ahead? He can fly into Cassie's cell and let her know we're coming. She might even be able to help from the inside."

"Fine," Nico says, with a shrug. "Go ahead, bat."

Greg gives Nico a nasty look, but it lasts a second too long, descending into confusion, then panic.

"What's wrong?" I ask.

"I...I can't shift," he says.

"Oh, bro..." Jordan stares at him. "That's not good. Have you tried prunes?"

"*SHIFT!*" I correct Jordan, who immediately looks down his shorts to make sure the favorite part of his anatomy hasn't changed without his knowledge.

Greg's face is red, all his effort focused onto something that should be natural... but it's just not happening.

"Greg," I reach out, but Nico grabs my hand.

"If he's sick, it might be catching."

Jordan takes a few steps back, then shifts to make sure he still can. The resulting panther trots farther away.

"Witch, we need you," Nico shouts to Hepa.

Hepa comes over to us and puts her hand on Greg's shoulder. "You're hot," she tells him. "If you can't shift, this is serious. We should go back."

"No," he says, droplets of sweat flying as he shakes his head. "What if Fern can't steal the keys again? I'll just stay here with you."

"I might have to put more effort into healing him if he gets worse," Hepa tells us. "I won't be able to protect us if you come back with anything on your tail."

"I'll stay too," Jordan says, back to human form. "I'll protect Greg and Hepa."

"Good," Nico says. "Back to a two-person mission. Edie?"

"Yes, let's go." I look at my team. Again, our mission is a disaster. Almost derailed before it's even started. "Be safe," I tell them.

Hoping this bad beginning isn't the end of us all, I follow Nico across the sands.

15

The air is utterly still, hot but dry. I lift my hair from my shoulders, tying it in a high pony. Nico's testosterone shot is still doing its work. I see his eyes wander over my briefly exposed midriff, and he instantly shifts into a werewolf, bolting out into the sands before coming back.

"Okay," he says, when he returns—he pauses to give himself a shake. Sand flies from his fur in all directions. Apparently satisfied, he changes back to his human form. It's funny how he doesn't look any less dangerous as a boy. He jerks his head toward me. "I can still shift. Now you."

"Huh?" I hadn't even considered that maybe I couldn't. I remember the panicked look on Greg's face, and feel a tickle of fear in my belly. *I just figured this out, please don't take it away.*

It hasn't been. I'm a mighty, glorious dragon in an instant. But my wings are a pale pearlescent hue, my worry and concern draining them of color.

I snap back into a girl.

"Good," Nico says. "I didn't want to say it in front of the

others, but if we were incapacitated, there would have been no option but to abort the mission."

"I would've gone in there as a human," I tell him.

He looks me up and down. It seems like this was some sort of test—and I passed it. "I thought so. Loyalty before all. It's my family motto."

Family motto? If my family had one it would've been, "If one person orders dessert, everyone shares it." I'm definitely getting the feeling that Nico's family is way more intense than mine had been. A pang of longing and loss stabs my gut. They're less frequent than they once were, but I don't think they'll ever go away completely. I've lost too much to simply get over it.

At least I've gotten better at pushing it aside and focusing on the task at hand. Which is what I do now.

"What's the plan, now that it's just the two of us again? We're going into a monster stronghold and we're highly outnumbered."

"Yes," Nico agrees. "But we've got advantages. I know the layout, and you're a dragon."

"Just two advantages?" I ask.

"Nope. There's one more." Nico's face gets tight and fierce. "I told them one day I'd kill them all. And I always keep my promises."

"Kill?" I hate to sound squeamish but the truth is—I *am* squeamish. I can't even look in the direction of the vampire's special blood fridge in the cafeteria; it makes my stomach turn.

Nico squints at me. "You've never killed before?"

"I have, but..." I hesitate; this isn't something I've mentioned to anyone else. Somehow, though, despite all his bullshit, I think Nico might understand. "I was a dragon and it was almost like...the dragon took control of me and I was watching it happen from the backseat."

"But at any time you could've demanded your dragon pull over and let you drive—and she would have, right?"

I stare at Nico in surprise. I thought he'd get it, but wow, he *really* gets it.

"Yeah. That." In a rush, I tell him the rest. "Since then, if I think about the killing, it's all fuzzy. Almost blurred out. I think my dragon is trying to protect me, so I don't have to deal what I did."

"It's not just trying to protect you," Nico explains. "It sounds like your dragon doesn't totally trust you. Have you ever locked your dragon out and refused to shift for a time?"

"Umm, yeah. You could say that." Nico obviously knows nothing about my past. How even after I knew that I was a shifter, I was afraid to find out what was inside. "I was afraid of my dragon. But then when the time came, I trusted her. I guess it makes sense that I now have to earn her trust."

"Yeah," Nico nods knowingly. "And your dragon's also probably really grossed out that you had a thing with a vampire."

"You think so? But..." Too late I notice the smile twitching at the corner of Nico's mouth. I whack his arm. "Jerk! I'm opening up about my inner animal stuff and you're making jokes at my expense."

He grabs hold of my hand. "You're right. I swear, it was all true, I just added the vampire thing, because it kills me to think of you with that guy. And also"—his hand tightens and I can feel him bristling—"it's all I can do to keep my inner wolf from tearing apart every vampire who crosses my path."

"Well, my dragon is definitely less blood-thirsty than your wolf," I say. "The only time it wants to kill is when my friends are being attacked. Not just because someone crosses my path. And I'd like to keep it that way. Which is why we're not going in there with a 'kill them all' attitude."

"You don't want blood on your hands?" Nico folds his arms over his chest "Fine. I'll come back later and finish the job on my own terms. But I'd love to hear how you expect to get Cassie out. The monsters are dug in there, and I mean that exactly—dug in. They've got a warren of tunnels, like ants. Now, if you wanted to do things the easy way, all you do is cough some fireballs down into one of those holes, and the flames will take out a good number of them."

"Yeah, that's not happening. Where is Cassie in that ant farm?"

"She's in a separate section. The cells only have two access tunnels, making them easier to guard."

I think for a minute. If only this place had Stormtroopers we could steal uniforms from...

Oh.

The little light bulb in my brain flicks on.

"I have a different plan." I say, turning toward Nico. "You're going to *hate* it."

16

"I thought being tortured in a monster prison was the lowest point of my life," Nico grouses. "But I was wrong."

"Be quiet," I shush him, "And keep your elbows tucked into your sides—you keep bumping me."

"Our teachers will be appalled when they hear about this. Kratos might quit on the spot."

"Seriously? The Greeks invented the whole Trojan horse thing."

"This is no horse."

Nico does have a point there. We are in fact stuffed into the inner cavity of a giant scorpion. The same one I drowned a few days ago.

When we returned to the portal to share my plan, Hepa and Jordan were playing tonsil hockey. I wasn't even mad. Greg was napping so what else would a horny panther and the witch who's obsessed with him do?

I cleared my throat and they parted, Jordan with a giant grin and Hepa looking sorta dreamy.

"Okay guys, pay attention," I told them as I laid out the plan.

Nico pointed out three separate times that this was all "Edie's crazy idea." Jordan, as usual, was totally into it. He helped me find and recover the scorpion's remains from the water. After that, all of us—except Greg—worked on digging out his water-softened innards.

Now, Nico and I creep ever closer to the compound with the scorpion's body giving us cover. It's like being inside of a nasty, putrid tank. So far what Nico described as "seriously the worst plan I've ever heard" is working exactly as I hoped. No one is sounding the alarm and rushing out to kill us. As far as the monsters know, their friend the scorpion is coming to the compound for his coffee break.

Even as I'm congratulating myself, a minotaur pops up from a tunnel entrance in the ground and stalks toward us. Nico growls low in his throat. I reach out and grab his bicep, my fingers curling around the tight muscle, begging him to just wait.

"What are you doing here?" The minotaur demands. "You've been tasked with guarding the portal. You can't leave."

As the minotaur gets closer I can see his expression change. His nostrils flair. "What's wrong with your...everything?"

"Now?" Nico whispers.

I sigh and agree reluctantly. "Now."

Nico slips out of the bottom of the carapace as I pop out my wings. They fit perfectly into the slots I carved on both sides of the scorpion's body, using my sharper than knives dragon claws.

"What the?" The minotaur says, his eyes widening as he takes in the wings.

I give a long eerie moan and flap my wings, making the whole scorpion's body shake. "I wear the chain I forged in life. I made it link by link, and yard by yard; I girded it on of my own free will, and of my own free will I wore it. Is its pattern strange to you?"

As I totally rip off Charles Dickens and do my best impression of a ghostly reanimated scorpion version of Jacob Marley, Nico shifts into his wolf form and zips away, staying close to the ground.

The minotaur's eyes narrow. Maybe his parents also forced him to read *A Christmas Carol*, or maybe like Greg, he's not buying the whole ghost scorpion thing. Even shivering with fever, Greg argued with nerdy conviction that a reanimated body is technically a zombie, not a ghost.

The minotaur snorts and then leaps, disappearing from my limited view. It doesn't take long to figure out where he went. He lands on my back, or the scorpion's back, which makes a terrible cracking noise.

Shit. I flap my wings and get enough air to shake him off. But in that time he must've sounded some sort of alarm, because monsters start to pour out from hidden holes all over the place.

Well, crap. Nico was right. Worst. Plan. Ever.

The minotaur once again hurtles toward me, face twisted with rage. I fly and twist, knocking him with the scorpion's tail. He rebounds quickly and with one swipe of his ax—the tail is gone.

Okay, time to ditch the disguise. I give a shake and a shimmy, but I'm stuck.

Monsters are roiling out of holes in the ground, like the ants Nico had promised they were. Everywhere I look, all I see are monsters, some reaching for bows, others throwing knives at me, some only shaking their fists.

Two arrows thunk into the scorpion's carapace. Then another and another. I know it's time to shift. Past time. But I'm nervous about letting my dragon take over. An arrow breaks through, piercing my leg. I scream and then I have no choice in the matter—my dragon bursts out of the scorpion shell and breaks free.

More arrows whiz by while harpies, flying in teams of three, come at me from both sides.

Fire rolls through my belly and I swoop down to take out the archers. Power, anger, fear, and fire are all brewing inside of me. As it comes to a boil, I expel it. Jets of fire erupt all around me.

I'd never tested my fire breathing abilities, and they are much, much stronger than I'd anticipated. Scorched sand is all that remains of where the archers once stood.

I blink at it, but my dragon is already wheeling around to face the first harpy team to reach me. They go for my wings, claws snatching at them. The third twists the arrow still embedded in my leg.

Inside I scream, outside my dragon roars. Together we fall, the ground coming fast.

The harpies break free right before I hit the ground.

Monsters of all types—more than I can name—are all over me in an instant. I scramble up, shaking them off and lighting them up, one by one, fighting for my life.

The last few run, realizing I won't go easily. I give chase, letting my hot breath lick their heels, wanting them to feel fear before they die. I can no longer tell where the dragon ends and I begin.

"Nooo!" A woman's voice pierces the chaos.

I twist my head to see a manticore running across the sand, a bundle in her arms. Her lion body stretches in great leaps while her human face twists in terror. The baby wails.

She stops, throwing herself in front of the minotaur I'd been chasing. Her wings fan out, wrapping around him.

I realize this must be the baby's father. And she's the guard whose birth created the distraction when Nico escaped.

Our eyes lock.

"Please," she says. Just that word and nothing more.

That bundle will grow up to be like its mother, maybe guarding a cell holding one of my friends. Maybe a cell that holds me.

Still...

I can't.

I turn away from her and shoot back up into the sky. I'd rather take my chances with another trio of harpies then hurt her. Almost immediately, I do. The first harpy dives into my space, slicing at my wings with a dagger. But I'm ready for that move this time. I snatch her in my claws, crush her quickly, and let what's left fall to the ground.

Another harpy comes after me and I pivot, diving low enough that my wings brush the sand, throwing up a wall behind me that goes into her eyes. Unfortunately, as I come around again, the same sand gets in my eyes too. I blink wildly, missing my human hands and the ability to rub my eyes.

I crash, rolling to a halt next to an opening in the sand—out of which comes Nico, Cassie on his back.

Nico is covered in blood, from his jaws to his great, heaving chest. Cassie is pale, but clutching him, her face a mask of fear. They bust through the remaining monsters, Nico tossing them from side to side with his jaws. I dive in close, plucking up Cassie and then Nico in each of my front talons. Nico instantly nips me.

It's more surprising than painful. "I'm trying to help you!" I dragon screech.

"I don't need help," he snarls back. "And I don't want to be carried!"

The third harpy comes at me.

"Fine," I say to Nico. "Have fun."

I throw him at the harpy. They slam into each other midair and it's immediately all claws and teeth.

I circle, worried that I might've just killed Nico. But there's no need for my concern.

Nico hits the ground, using the dead harpy as a cushion. Within moments, he's back on his feet, launching himself at another victim.

High above, I can see a clear path for Nico's escape.

"Nico!" I roar down to him. "This way!"

He glances up at me for the barest instant—just enough for me to know he heard me. And then he turns his back on me, his teeth latching onto the next victim.

That's when I get it. He's not leaving. Nico Tralano is staying to tear out more throats.

I wait a moment longer, wanting to believe I'm wrong.

In my claw, I feel Cassie sobbing, her tears running down my talon as I finally turn away and fly us back to the portal.

17

I
t's dark by the time Nico returns. He limps into view,
howls, and collapses.

Hepa is busy tending Greg who has gotten steadily
worse. Cassie cried herself to sleep. Which leaves Jordan
and me keeping watch. After Nico falls into the sand, we
exchange glances.

"He's not getting back up," I say.

"Yep. Looks like we gotta get the grumpy bastard,"
Jordan agrees.

Hepa already treated where the arrow pierced my leg
and the other more superficial scrapes and bruises. I'm not
in terrible pain, but I'm also in no condition to help carry a
werewolf. And even though Jordan is a big guy, he doesn't
have anywhere near Nico's mass. He ends up dragging Nico
through the silt. Clumps of bloody sand are left behind in
his wake.

I gently shake Cassie awake, while Hepa wafts something under Nico's noise. His one good eye is crusted closed
with blood. A wound on his head oozes. But after a few
minutes, Jordan is able to help him to his feet.

Hepa throws the portal key into the fountain. Jordan and Nico stagger through the portal together. Finally, Hepa, Cassie, and I surround Greg, each ready to catch him if he falls.

He grins through lips cracked with fever. "Surrounded by all these beautiful ladies. I'm living the dream."

We arrive back on campus nearly a whole day after we left. I half expect Themis to be waiting at the portal to bust us. But even though it's midday here, it's eerily quiet. Even if they didn't notice that all of us were missing—which is unlikely, as there should at least be people in the quad. But when we make our way through it's like a ghost town.

"Something's not right," Jordan says.

This isn't him being unusually astute. There's a giant green sphere of light shining up into the sky from the middle of campus.

"That's a quarantine light," Hepa says. She looks at Greg who can barely remain upright. "Jordan, run to the infirmary, tell them we need help. *Now*."

Jordan immediately shifts into his sleek panther form and runs off. I turn to where Hepa is trying to make Greg comfortable on a patch of grass, but she waves me away.

"You need to stay away. Don't touch him at all."

I turn my attention to Cassie, who looks like she's in shock. Her eyes dart around before finally focusing on me.

"Are you okay?" I ask. "Are you hurt?"

She shakes her head. I don't know if she's saying she's not okay, or that she's not hurt. I go to hug her but she shies away. "So much death," she whispers.

"Cassie!" Merilee's voice echoes through the quad.

Cassie's mother bounds across the space and scoops Cassie up in her arms. Both of them collapse into a heap of tears.

"I was afraid I'd never see you again," Merilee says. "But I had a spell put on the portals to alert me if you stepped a foot on campus."

"I saw this. You and me together at this portal, exactly like this," Cassie tells her. "I knew I just had to be patient."

"I missed you. I'm so glad you're safe and sound." Merilee rocks Cassie back and forth.

I look away, feeling like I'm imposing on a private moment. But also a little bit like Cassie stole *my* moment. *I* was the one who was supposed to be reunited with my mother. The hugging and crying and all the rest of it—I wanted that.

I still do.

Hepa steers me away from them. "Give them some space. If you want to help someone, go see how much of that werewolf's blood is his own."

I turn to Nico. He's still in wolf form, barely able to keep on his feet. It's clear that he won't remain upright long. I hurry over and then am not sure what to do.

"Nico, lie down," I say, once again resorting to treating him like a dog.

He gives a short bark that sounds like a laugh, and then slowly sinks to the ground. With a soft whimper he curls into himself. I put a hand on his back, his fur coarse and stiff with blood. Then suddenly that same hand is resting on warm human skin.

I am once again dealing with a naked Nico. Quickly, I pull my pack off and yank out a blanket. Nico takes it word-lessly and wraps it around his lower half. Now that all the bruising and wounds are easily visible, it definitely looks bad...but not deadly.

Once again, Nico will survive.

He turns his head to look at me, his eyes glazed with

pain. "Did everyone make it back? I didn't..." He stops and shakes his head, ruefully. "You shouldn't have waited on me."

"We weren't gonna just leave you behind."

"Why not?"

The question floors me. "Because...I know what it's like to be left behind."

I know Nico thinks I'm talking about my last mission and my team going through the portal without me, but that was nothing compared to the way I felt after dad and grandma died. Then when I couldn't find my mom or Mavis and they didn't contact me—I felt abandoned. Lost.

It was devastating. I wouldn't wish that on anyone.

Nico's one eye is fixed on me, steadily glowing, until finally he blinks. "I guess that's now two that I owe you, Edie."

"That's not why I helped you."

"Yeah, I know." Nico pauses as if weighing his next words. "You almost make me think that being soft is a good thing."

"Soft?" I jerk away from him. "Just because I didn't go after those monsters like a-a-a—"

"Animal?"

"No," I spit the word at him. I glance at Cassie and echo her words. "So much death. Like you were the real monster there."

Nico's eye widens and then his face goes hard as he turns away. Maybe I should be happy with getting the last word in, but now that we're talking about it—I want answers.

"Did you kill everyone? Did you kill your prison guard and her baby?"

Nico's shoulders stiffen. "You didn't even know them."

"Are they dead now?"

He spins around, teeth bared. "No. Okay? She was always nice to me, so—" With a sigh he puts his face into his hands, like the effort of holding his head up is too much. "No mercy. No regrets. That's how my mother raised me. If she knew I'd spared anyone…"

"Your mother sounds like—"

Before I can finish that thought, Jordan arrives back with a trio of healers running fast behind him. As they get closer to Greg, one of the healers grabs the back of Jordan's shirt.

"Into one of the isolation rooms. Now." Nico and I earn a quick glance. "Both of you too." Then their focus turns to Greg.

"How long has he been sick?" asks the older woman in charge. I've seen her around the infirmary. She's Metis, the Titan who teaches healing to the witches and warlocks.

"Since yesterday afternoon," Hepa replies, her tone crisp and professional. "He was seemingly fine, although later he reported that he'd been suffering from loose bowels."

Greg groans, whether from pain or from having his BM habits reported in front of everyone—it's hard to say.

"He realized he couldn't shift," Hepa continues, "and then almost immediately the symptoms began."

"When?" the healer asks, her voice sharp.

"Uh…" Well, I guess with Cassie back, our mission yesterday isn't exactly a secret anymore. "It would've been yesterday afternoon."

"Dear gods," the head healer says, looking stricken as she studies Greg. "Campus cases didn't break out until very early this morning." She looks up at the two healers standing over Greg.

"I think we just found patient zero."

———

W e finally rescued Cassie and now I can't even speak with her. Her mom led her to the records' building and before I could follow, I was also whisked away.

All of the shifters are quarantined. Whatever this disease is ripping through campus, it appears only to affect the shifters. Greg was taken away to the infirmary for tests. Since Jordan, Nico, and I aren't showing symptoms, we're asked to wait in the amphitheater until everyone can be tested. With Nico injured, Hepa volunteered to keep an eye on him. I'm sure her wanting to be next to Jordan has absolutely nothing to do with it.

Within the amphitheater area we are sectioned into shifters that have been in contact with the infected, and those that haven't. Fern is talking to the students in the very small 'no contact' group. I wave to get her attention and she walks over.

She is clearly exhausted. She probably hasn't slept since she took one for the team and distracted Hermes with talk of sex. She looks around, then casts a sound shield.

"What is happening?" I ask. "What's wrong with Greg? Is it really a shifter disease? Do we all have it?"

"Whoa, one question at a time," she tells me. "And *I* go first. Tell me about your mission—did you get Cassie?"

She must have really been busy if she didn't hear the news. I relay everything. When we get to the fight, I falter, but I tell it like it happened. By the end I'm choked up while tears roll silently down Fern's face.

"All that death..." I say. "I know it's war, but I wasn't prepared for it."

Fern wipes her face. "You killed Ocypete," she says quietly. "I thought you hated the monsters. I thought you were just like everyone else here."

"I do hate the monsters!"

Fern's expression shifts to one of disappointment. I'm surprised by how much that hurts me.

"War is death," she tells me. "I have to get back to my patients. You'll get an update soon." She pauses, her lips tight. "And for the record. *I* don't hate them."

There it is. She admitted it out loud.

"Wait!" I grab hold of her arm. I know this isn't a good time to ask, but there may never be a good time. "Ocypete told me you were one of hers."

I'd thought it was a lie—a tactic to get me on her side.

Fern's eyes widen and her lips go white.

"So, it's true?" I ask.

"I didn't want anyone to get hurt. I didn't understand what following orders from Ocypete would mean." Her shining brown eyes stare into mine. "I just wanted this war to end. I'm a healer! I thought I was helping when I snuck the portal key to her..."

It takes a minute for me to fully understand what she's saying to me.

"*You* gave Ocypete the key to bring the monsters here the night of the Spring Fling?"

"Yes," Fern nods, tears falling. "And people died because of it."

"Why did you mess with the rest of the keys?"

"That was an accident. I was so nervous that I would get caught, I dropped all the keys and put them back randomly." After a long moment, she asks, "Are you going to turn me in?"

I don't know what to say. Fern just confessed to being a traitor. Sweet, sincere, helpful Fern. She's working for the monsters. And I know well enough what the gods do to traitors—you have the choice of death by fire or flood. Burn or drown. I shudder, not wanting to send my friend to that fate, no matter what she did.

"Can you stop now? Pity's dead. Can you just be on our side and pretend you always were?"

"Edie," Fern lets my name out on a sigh. "It's so much more complicated than that."

Before I can ask anything else she pops the sound bubble and walks away.

I let her go. There's really nothing else to say anyway.

I turn to Hepa and Jordan, who are whispering over Nico's sleeping form. It looks intense so I keep my distance and study the room.

Waiting is the worst. Especially when you have a bunch of shifters who are basically wild animals. Everyone is on edge, and accusations are flying, cat-shifters blaming were-wolves for the plague, bird-shifters blaming cat-shifters, and those who dare to defend anyone outside of the animal group is getting attacked by both sides. But underneath it all is pure panic; suddenly, shifters can't shift. They want to know why—and who to blame.

I lean closer to Hepa, and whisper, "Where is Greg being kept?"

"Isolation," she tells me, scanning the crowd. "For his own safety. When Marguerite tasted his blood—"

"What?!" I shriek, and she shushes me quickly. "That's how we're testing. The vamps can taste the infection. Losing the ability to shift is one of the last symptoms; we can't have infected shifters wandering around campus spreading the plague, just because they haven't reached that point yet. So the vamps are helping out and that's not—"

But Hepa doesn't have to tell me that's not going well. There's a panicked scream from the front of the room. The crowd shifts, giving me a clear view of the shifter who just had her blood tested by a vamp. She tries to shift into her cat form, but gets stuck halfway. Still, her claws are vicious as she swipes at the vamp, spit flying from her jaws.

Two other vamps jump in at the same time that several shifters pile on. Behind me I hear, "Oh hell no."

I turn to find Nico awake and staggering to his feet. He staggers forward and I'm pretty certain it's going to get all Hunger Games-y in here, but with a bolt of lightning, Zee and Themis appear.

Themis steps forward to speak first. "Students, as you all know, a sickness has infected several shifters. Please be assured they are getting the best care possible and we have confidence they will fully recover."

"Yeah, but will they shift again?" someone calls out to my left.

Interrupting Themis is almost unheard of; that someone would do it shows how high tensions are right now.

She glances toward the interrupter as if making note of it for later retribution, and then continues.

"Thanks to the discovery of patient zero, we now believe the sickness can be traced to a bug bite. However, we are still uncertain whether or not the disease can be passed from one shifter to another, so the quarantine will remain in effect until every student has been tested. Furthermore, a magical fumigation will take place shortly. I have been warned that it will be a bit pungent, however it is the most effective way of safeguarding our native insect species while ensuring that all foreign invaders are swiftly exterminated. Now, if you will all be patient, you will each be tested one by one—"

"One moment!" Zee steps forward, nearly elbowing Themis aside, although she neatly sidesteps him before he can make contact. "You forgot the most important thing, Themis."

"Did I?" she answers wryly.

Zee, as usual, doesn't seem to hear her. "Sickness. Disease. Death." He pauses for dramatic effect. "No one wants that at their school. And certainly not at Mount Olympus Academy. We can't settle for simply being the strongest. And the smartest. We also need to be the healthiest. And that starts at birth. No, *before* birth. It starts in the bedroom. With whomever you choose to bring into the bedroom. Or the gardens. Or in the library hidden between the stacks." Zee shakes his head, looking a little confused, but then his eyes light up and he's off again.

"What I'm saying is, it doesn't matter where you perform the act, it matters how well you perform the act." He stops and frowns. "No! It matters with whom you perform the act. Well, how well is important too. So, to recap, first choose the right person. Second, make sure you do it well. Third, be willing to accept helpful feedback. We can all learn and grow and improve. Why just in the last half century, thanks to a lover's advice, I learned—"

"Zee," Themis interrupts. "You're getting a little off track here and I'm not sure the students fully understand what you're telling them."

It's true. I'm completely lost. And a little amused. Also a lot mortified. Although no one dares to actually laugh aloud. Mr. Zee is too mercurial. He might laugh along, or he might throw a lightning bolt to teach you a lesson.

"What I'm saying," Mr. Zee booms, "is there will be no more interspecies relations. Vampires will stick with vampires. Witches and warlocks with witches and warlocks. Shifters with shifters—of their same type."

A rumble goes through the crowd at this last part. It's

one thing to cut the dating pool into thirds, but for rarer shifters—like me—this will eliminate the dating pool entirely.

"ENOUGH!" Thunder shakes the room and everyone's hair stands on end as an electrical currents zip over our heads. "These types of sicknesses are born of bad blood—"

"Zee, I already told them we believe it was a bug bite—"

Zee puts a finger in Themis' face. "Yes, the free love bug! But no more. As I am god, I declare it so, any students caught cross-canoodling will be sterilized."

There are gasps around me. Themis blinks hard. For her that's the equivalent of having her mouth drop open. But after a moment she says in a soft voice, "It was declared and it will be so."

And that's it. They leave as quickly as they arrived.

The moment they're gone everyone starts talking at once. Some clearly see it as an opportunity. Two of Greg's close friends high five.

"No more competing with vamps for chicks!"

Others are more concerned with their lower extremities. Like Jordan for instance. He has both hands over his crotch. "Nobody's neutering me. No way. No how."

Hepa rolls her eyes. "Jordan, it would be magical steril-ization, not castration."

"Uh-uh." He shakes his head. "No one messes with my junk. Except in a sexy way."

"And what about me, Jordan?" Hepa puts her hands on her hips. "Remember my soft gentle hands? And how they belong to a witch and not a shifter?"

Jordan's face goes soft as Hepa waves her hands in his face. "You have great hands. I'll miss them."

I shake my head. Did they have "we might all die" sex

while waiting for us to return with Cassie? On second thought, I really don't want to know.

"You'll *miss* them?!" If Hepa was a dragon shifter, fire would definitely have come out of her mouth with that one.

"Babe!" Jordan says. "I'm not getting neutered for you. I mean, that would kind of undermine the point, right?"

"You're a coward." Hepa tells Jordan and then stalks over to where Nico has returned to his makeshift sickbed. I expect Nico to be happier than anyone about this announcement. Clearly, Mr. Zee is seizing the reins of power once more.

But he looks concerned more than anything else. Our eyes meet and he gives a one-shouldered shrug, as if to say, "what can you do?"

I turn away and nearly collide with Jordan. His hands haven't moved from their protective positioning around his crotch.

"Edie, I'm afraid."

I reach out and pat his back. "I know, buddy. We all are."

18

A week later everything is back to normal...and yet not normal at all. The quarantine on non-infected shifters has been lifted, but the inter-species dating ban is still in effect. Relationships have broken up, and not just romantic ones. Some hard words have passed between friends with the arrival of the plague, and having the vamps test blood wasn't the best move on the healers' part.

I was cleared of the sickness and sent back to my room where Tina was freaking out because Vee wasn't reacting well to the witches' fumigation spell. She bared her fangs and hissed at me, "This is all your fault, Swamper."

My roommate hating me was definitely normal. Almost comforting, actually. But Vee's head was hanging low, and while it's hard to develop a close personal relationship with a plant, I had been feeding Vee all summer. I didn't like that she looked...sick.

Everything is different and the same all at once. I meet Cassie for our normal walk down to the dining hall. But when we got there, Greg wasn't in his usual seat. The initial fever has passed, but he and the eight other students who fell ill still can't shift. One girl, a lion shifter, is stuck in her animal form. She loses more words every day. There are worries they might have to cage her if the animal part of her nature eclipses the human.

Cassie's also not back to normal. Much like the poor girl stuck as a lion, Cassie seems to still be stuck in her prison cell. I find myself desperately searching for topics that might interest her, but also not remind her of all the bad stuff that happened. Cassie saw her boyfriend decapitated, and then gods knew what else in the monster stronghold. Usually I tell Cassie everything. But the other day when I was bummed because most students received care packages, it seemed insensitive to grouse about it in front of Cassie.

It's an unsolvable problem—I don't want to talk about the bad stuff, and the good stuff feels too insensitive. So I settle for not talking. Just me and Cassie sitting side by side, eating silently.

At least summer classes are starting today. It'll be nice to have that distraction.

There's been enough drama on campus to keep people talking, but the impending arrival of Maddox Tralano (a.k.a. Nico's mommy) has still been a hot topic. Cassie and I have our first class with her today.

Cassie and I stand to empty our trays. I have to guide her by the elbow, like she's forgotten the layout of the dining hall.

"Ready for..." I glance at my schedule, forgetting the official name of the class. "Real World Applications for Assassination. That's...cheery." I fold the paper, sorry I said anything. Cassie doesn't need to be reminded of killing.

"Hello? Edie?" Someone is yelling my name on the green, a voice I don't recognize. I turn to find Larissa Golov

—Val's fiancée—waving at me. She crosses the grass, her long gauzy skirt blowing around her perfect legs. I get a sudden image of Val positioned in between them and have to turn away, fire shifting in my gut.

I affix a smile before I turn back. My instinct is to dislike her, but Larissa is pleasant, which is almost an unheard of trait for a vampire.

Besides, even if Val and I wanted to be together—we couldn't. His family is strict about pure vampire blood. Plus Tina has reveled in telling me every night how lucky Val is to have arranged a marriage with the Golovs.

Also, interspecies dating is now banned on campus.

Oh, and the whole girls squabbling over a boy thing is kinda gross so...I guess I might as well be nice to this girl.

"Hey," I call, waving to her. She joins me and Cassie, wrapping an arm around my friend to give her a one-armed side hug.

"I am so sorry for all you've been through," she says, her voice quiet and sweet. "If there's anything I can do..."

Astonishingly, Cassie lays her head against Larissa's shoulder.

"Thank you," she says—the first words I've heard out of her all day. And they're to Val's fiancée.

Nice.

The fire in my gut rolls again, but I stifle it. I should just be glad to hear Cassie's voice.

We file into the amphitheater. The entire campus is enrolled in this class, and there are more students in here right now than I've seen together since...well, since Tina's friend Jenn was turned into a pile of ash, burned to death by Ocypete.

Larissa waves and I follow her gesture to find Val across the aisle with his sister and her crew. Larissa cups her hands around her mouth and shouts, "I am going to sit here with my friends!"

He nods and turns away. Tina shoots me a dirty look, like I've brainwashed Larissa or something.

There are whispers all around us. Most people talk about the shifters who are still quarantined in the infirmary, unable to shift into their animal forms. I catch the name of the poor girl who is stuck as a lion—Rochelle—more than once, but she's almost an afterthought. The name being tossed around the most is Maddox Tralano.

"Who?" Larissa asks. "Why is this name coming up so often?"

"She's our teacher for this class, a guest instructor," I tell her.

"Maddox Tralano," Larissa repeats. "What a pretty name."

"Don't tell her that," Cassie says, a little bit of life coming into her. "She won't accept a compliment from a vampire. On second thought, don't even talk to her. Don't call attention to yourself in her presence."

Larissa's perfect brows come together, a pretty pout on her lips. I glance at them quickly, wondering if Val has kissed her. I mean, I assume he has. They're getting married so—a small fireball pops out of my mouth, making Larissa and Cassie jump.

"Sorry," I say quickly. "That chili at lunch had a real kick."

"Why shouldn't I talk to her?" Larissa asks.

"Oh, Maddox *hates* vampires," Cassie says, sounding a little like her old self at the chance to share some gossip. "I mean, she's like, half the reason there's so much bad blood around the Academy."

"What?" I ask. "Why?"

"Remember the Wall of Weeping?" Cassie asks me. I nod. How could I forget?

Apparently, years ago Themis thought it would be a good idea to ensure *everyone* on campus mourned when a student died in battle. It was supposed to bring students together, strengthen the bond of *us against them*, uniting them against the monsters.

"But it went wrong, like bad," Cassie is explaining to Larissa. "Maddox was on her mourning shift with a vamp and well...the Academy ended up with more than one dead student on their hands."

"Oh my gods," I say. "That was her?"

I knew the story, how a werewolf tore a vamp to pieces at the Wall. But I didn't know it was Nico's mom.

"How are they even letting her come back to campus?" I ask. "And *teaching*?"

Larissa is nodding with me, but Cassie only shrugs. "Mr. Zee made a proclamation. My mom says that Maddox was always a favorite of his. And what Mr. Zee says, goes."

Larissa shakes her head. "My family warned me not to associate with...shifters." She lowers her voice, like it's a bad word. "But I think you are very nice, Edie."

"Thank you," I tell her, ashamed at how much I wanted to hate her.

Suddenly, there's a sharp rapping at the podium. Themis is there, eyeing the crowd of students. "Everyone," she says, bringing the room to order. "I'm here to introduce you to—"

But Themis doesn't get to introduce anybody. A tall, dark, lean woman saunters onto the stage, announcing her own self.

"I'm Maddox Tralano," she says, her voice filling the entire space.

Anybody that hadn't been sitting up straight is now. All

eyes are locked on her, and not just because she has a commanding presence. She's also gorgeous in a way that goes beyond hair styles or clothing choices. It's pure animal magnetism. Nico has it too, but with Maddox the magnetism is way more intense. I can't take my eyes off of her.

"Our official sessions will start in the morning," Maddox continues. "But I want to make sure everyone understands what we're doing here."

Several students glance at one another, like they'd never really thought about it.

"We are AT WAR!" Maddox yells, thumping the podium.

Beside me, Larissa flinches, and Cassie lets out a little gasp.

"War is ugly," Maddox says, now pacing the stage. "Ugly like the monsters we fight—harpies and manticores and minotaurs. War is death and destruction—the deaths of our enemies! The destruction of their way of life. War is what we bring to the doorsteps of those who have persecuted us for generations."

There are still confused whispers, but also yells of agreement from the crowd as the students warm up to her pep talk.

"How many of you have been on a mission?" Maddox asks, scanning the crowd for hands. "Don't be shy. Raise your hands. Be proud of your service, and I thank you all for it."

Hesitantly, I put my hand in the air.

"The rest of you, look around. I want that number doubled!" She glares at the crowd, daring those who didn't raise their hands to meet her gaze. "Now, how many of you have killed?"

I snap my hand back, uncertain. I don't want to be

praised for killing. I spot Nico in the front row, arm raised high.

Maddox looks down at him. I expect some maternal gleam of affection, but instead all I see is cold satisfaction. "Be proud of your abilities. Everyone else, look around. I want that number tripled!" she shouts, and there's a roar of excitement.

"You don't win a war by going to dances," she goes on. "You don't win a war by going to classes. You don't win a war by just being a student at Mount Olympus Academy." She stops, pausing for effect.

"How do you win a war?" she asks the crowd.

"Killing!" someone shouts. Was it Nico? Maddox nods in agreement.

"I'm not here to treat like you all like students—like children," she says, giving everyone a final, grim look.

"I'm here to train you to be soldiers. The soldiers who finally *win* and end this war, once and for all!"

The students' applause is deafening.

19

"Well, that was something," I say to Tina when I return to the dorms.

Tina and I aren't exactly close, but since it's certain now that I won't be polluting her family's pure vampire bloodline by dating her brother, she's been a little more chill. And by a little more chill I mean that she hasn't elongated her fangs at me in almost a week.

"You ran out of there pretty fast," I say, tossing my school issue jacket onto my bed. "I'm guessing you felt the same way I did during Maddox Tralano's...rally?" There's no other word for it. She was gathering the troops and firing up their blood.

Tina doesn't answer me. She must still be mad that Larissa sat with me during Tralano's speech. I'm probably in trouble now.

"I think she's totally nuts," I go on. "And did you know that she's the one who—Tina?"

My roommate is lying in bed, the covers pulled around her protectively. Like a true vamp, Tina doesn't sleep. When she is "on" her bed, she's usually floating above the blankets.

But she's in the fetal position right now, and shaking like a leaf.

"Tina?" I walk over to her, noticing something on the floor between our beds.

"Gross!" I use a tissue to lift up a tiny, dead scorpion. "Oh my gods! Tina, did you see this?"

She doesn't respond. There's sweat pouring off her brow, and her mouth is locked shut as she convulses slightly, like she's fighting the urge to puke. Oh gods. I've heard that when vampires puke it gets...messy.

I gingerly wrap the scorpion inside the tissue, being careful not to crush it.

"I've got to get this to the infirmary," I tell her. "They said the plague was started by a bug bite, that's why they fumigated. This thing must have come through the portal with us when—"

"I'm not sick," Tina says, her mouth barely opening to let the words out.

"Um...you look pretty sick," I tell her.

She does. For the first time in my life I can actually say a vampire looks like shit. Tina's skin is waxy, her hair sweat soaked and...only blonde. Her green streaks are gone. That's weird. I've never seen her without them.

"I'm not sick," Tina repeats, but a little runnel of blood escapes from one of her nostrils as she says it.

"Tina..." I say, approaching her cautiously. "You honestly do not look good. I think you need to come to the infirmary with me."

"*I'm not sick*," she says again, and tries to show her fangs, but they only erupt halfway. She grips my wrist, squeezing. Even her freaky vampire strength is gone. "I *do not* have the plague."

"Of course you don't," I say. "I mean, duh. You're a pure-blood vampire, and the plague only affects shift—"

I pause as things click into place.

Tina, so concerned with keeping up appearances.

The time I caught her pulling her hand through her hair and adding a streak of green, which Cassie said was a shifter trick.

Her preoccupation with keeping Val away from me, and having him marry someone with a great vampire pedigree. She's trying to protect him from the truth.

Oh. My. Gods.

Tina's gaze meets mine, bright, burning, begging.

Tina isn't a pureblooded vampire.

That means Val isn't either...

Does Larissa know? And if not, would she still want to marry him?

———

I hurry to the infirmary. A witch at the quarantine area stops me, but when I show her what I'm holding she goes white. Then she snaps, "Follow me to the infirmary immediately."

I know the witches are under a ton of pressure right now with the outbreak and since it's where I was going anyway, I resist the urge to snark back.

Inside the lab, there's normal looking equipment, like microscopes, but also bubbling cauldrons. Next to an eye wash station is a stone table carved with runes.

I spot Metis, the healer in charge, and make my way over to her. She's busy looking through a microscope, then reading an incantation from a book.

"Excuse me..." Her sharp eyes focus on me.

For a moment I lose my words. I'm not prepared for the weight of her gaze. I know she's a Titan, older than the Greek gods themselves. Her presence is intimidating, her eyes bright with ancient knowledge.

She looks me up and down. "You're the dragon?"

"Yes," I say, and add a "ma'am" for good measure.

She humphs. "You're tall, and have ample muscle tone. If you weren't a shifter I would think you'd be more suited to my daughter's academy."

Wait, there are other Academies? Of course there are.

"Your daughter?" I ask stupidly. Maybe I should spend more time studying.

"My daughter Athena. She is the headmistress of Amazon Academy. I'm sure she'd love to get her greedy hands on you, but no shifters allowed. Not like Hades and his Underworld Academy. He'll take anyone. Anyone dead, anyway."

I hate to interrupt but I feel like Metis is losing interest in me. "I...I found this. On my dorm room floor."

Again her full attention snaps to me and I feel like I'm a specimen under her microscope. But then I hand her the dead scorpion and it's like I'm no longer in the room. Or even the same planet. Metis carefully places it in a specimen bag and then calls for the other witches and warlocks in the lab.

Just like that—I'm forgotten. By everyone.

They huddle around the insect, so solemn it almost looks like they're in the midst of a funeral. Then one of the warlocks asks, "Who had scorpion in the office pool?"

"I think it was Rose."

"And maybe Warren too."

"Definitely not me. I went with a killer bee.".

"I thought mosquito was a winner."

"You and half the staff here."

"Enough." Metis almost whispers the word, but immediately everyone goes silent. "My choice was a loser in the pool and thus my interest in this topic has ended. Let us move on. This ugly insect which has apparently cost me several gold coins in a fortune too vast to be counted may be the answer to our patients next door. Let us discuss this further."

Another spirited discussion erupts with wizards and witches talking over one another.

One of the warlocks says there's no way it's the cause, as scorpion venom only incapacitates, but someone else hazards that it could be a bio-weapon created by the monsters. Then they get into a hypothetical argument about what the goal of a bio weapon that only affects shifters might be. It quickly gets technical and way over my head.

Finally, one kindly witch notices I'm still there and tells me I can leave.

I back away and head down the hall, to the room with the quarantined shifters. As soon as I found that scorpion, a plan to sneak inside was already forming in my head. If the plague was caused by that scorpion, I won't catch it by checking on my fellow classmates.

I spot Greg and, in the bed next to him, surprisingly, Jordan. I hadn't seen him at the rally but I didn't realize...

I rush to them, circumventing the lion in the middle of the room. They brought in a cage for Rochelle and she's pacing back and forth, snarling occasionally. When I reach Greg he gives me a sad smile.

"Not you too, Edie?" he asks.

"No, no...I just wanted to check on you. And Jordan, I didn't even know you'd gotten sick. What happened?" I ask.

He shakes his head. "I woke up this morning and when I

went out for my run I couldn't shift. I just...nothing like this has ever happened to me before, I swear." He looks on the verge of tears. "This is the first time I've been unable to perform ..."

I hug him, then hug Greg and sit at the foot of his bed.

"The worst thing," Jordan is saying, "is that you don't truly know what you have until it's gone. I mean, when something is just there all the time, you take it for granted." His eyes go to Hepa who is helping another patient.

"That's really deep," I say.

"And who is gonna want to bang a shifter who can't shift?" he asks.

Greg actually laughs. "Okay, he's back now. Hi, Jordan."

"How are you really?" I ask Greg.

"Bored. Mostly. There's talk about making us—the infected—go home. Permanently."

"They're gonna kick you out of school?" I say in a voice way too loud for the sick room. Quickly, I modulate my volume. "I won't let that happen." Although I don't know what I could do to stop it.

Greg shrugs. "Well, if we're shifters who can't shift, we're actually just humans." He stops, apparently remembering that I couldn't shift for most of last year. "Sorry, Edie. But it's true."

I spot Fern and drop my voice to a whisper.

"Look, I'm pretty sure I found the cause...a baby scorpion. It must have slipped through the portal, that's why I got stuck on the other side. Remember that bite on your back, Greg? I think it rode through with you."

"But that's only four living things," Jordan argues, and I see that he's used his fingers to calculate. "The portal key was set for five to return, including your mom."

I don't know what to say to that, and I hate the reminder

that our entire mission failed and left my mother gods knew where.

"Um... guys?" Greg says. "I think I know why it closed. Five things *did* pass through. I sort of kind of might have snatched a beetle out of the air right before we left. And if I didn't masticate—"

"Whoa dude, don't beat yourself up." Jordan says. "Everybody masticates. It's normal and natural."

"Chew, Jordan," I tell him, and he apparently takes it as a command because he immediately starts doing it. "Masticate *means* chew," I clarify.

"Ohhhh," Jordan says. "Well, yeah. I guess that would do it then. If Greg hadn't crunched down on his snack yet and there was a scorpion riding in on him—"

"Great, so it's definitely all my fault," Greg says, tears sprouting.

"Maybe," I tell him. "But if it hadn't happened, I never would have found Nico, and he would've died out in that desert."

"I am totally blaming you for that one, then," Jordan says to Greg. "Nico is a total dick."

"Oh come on, he's not that bad," Greg argues. "He's come and visited us almost every day."

"What?" I'm shocked. "How did he get away with that?"

"He snuck in." Jordan rolls his eyes. "He said no one keeps him out when he wants in. It sounded sorta sexual."

"Jordan, everything sounds sexual to you," I point out.

"Okay fine," he shrugs, giving that one to me. "But when I asked if he was afraid of getting sick he said, 'Tralanos don't let themselves get sick. It's a weakness.'"

"Yeah," Greg adds. "I'm kinda getting the sense that his mom is a piece of work."

"Oh she is, just wait until you get better and have to start attending her class."

"*If* we get better," Greg corrects, looking gloomy once more.

"You will," I assure him. "I gave the scorpion to the healers. I'm sure it'll be only a matter of time before they have a cure."

"Yeah," Greg's face lights up. "I'm sure you're right."

"I gotta go, but I'll come back as soon as I can." I hurry over to Fern. "I need you to come with me. Now."

"Is this about the mons...?" The words die on her lips when she sees my face. "Edie, what's wrong?"

I pull her out of the infirmary but we're stopped by a group of vamps. Val is among them. Today his shirt features a merman and says, *Be Mermazing.* I think of Darcy and don't know whether to laugh or cry. "You know the rules, girls. No one leaves without being tested."

Val steps forward, his expression as unreadable as ever.

I sigh and give him my hand. He takes it gently, his eyes meeting mine.

I forgot how cold he is. Cold in a way that I find really hot.

Slowly, he leans forward, exposing his fangs. He bites into my wrist.

The first time I had this done, they assured me that a bite alone couldn't turn someone into a vampire, there's a whole process involving the victim willingly also drinking some of the vampire's blood. And...yeah, ugh. I'm not doing that.

And yet I have to admit, there's a strange, pleasurable sensation from a vampire bite. A rush. I gasp, trying not to let the good feeling get to me. But because it's Val all my other emotions are mixed up and I can't help but blush, wondering what it would feel like for him to bite me other places.

"Clear," one of the vamps says of Fern. I guess they're still testing the witches to make sure that it doesn't jump species, or...remembering Tina's mixed blood, I entertain the thought that maybe Mr. Zee has the vamps doing the blood test to sniff out any Moggies.

Val raises his head and keeps staring at me, still holding my wrist. There's so much I want to say to him. To ask him. He doesn't even know that I'm aware of his secret. He doesn't know that I don't care if he's a pure vampire. I wouldn't care if he was part poodle.

"Clear," he echoes.

He drops my wrist. The bite is already fading; a vampire's saliva can actually have healing properties if they choose to excrete it. Val walks away and I stare after him, wondering if I should tell him about Tina. No. I'll wait and see what Fern thinks. Maybe I'm overreacting and Tina just has a bad summer cold or something.

"Edie," Fern prompts and the trance is broken.

In hushed whispers I explain to Fern along the way. I don't think she truly believes me until she sees Tina for herself. She gets right to business, taking Tina's temperature.

Tina opens her bleary eyes. "I didn't ask you to bring me a healer."

"She won't tell anyone," I promise her. "It was this or the infirmary."

Fern looks at me. "I'm good at keeping secrets."

"This isn't affecting her like it is the shifters," Fern tells me. "She looks a lot worse off than the other infected. Maybe..." Fern hesitates. "Maybe she's not a purebred vampire?"

Tina hisses at us. "Don't you dare say that aloud."

"No one else is here," I assure her.

"You and she are already too many! If anyone finds out, our family will be ruined." Her eyes go dark and small red droplets spring from them. She's crying blood.

This freaks me out so much I try to make her angry again. Anything other than her quiet desperation.

"Okay then, well in that case, I'll just let you die."

She looks up at me, sees that I'm not serious, and actually laughs weakly.

"What do you think?" I ask Fern.

"She needs a blood transfusion. Preferably from a pure-blooded vampire."

"How the hell are we going to...wait, can you ask Marguerite?" I hadn't even bothered to check in with Fern and find out if they were still together after the proclamation. To be fair, I was also thinking about how Fern let the monsters on campus, so neither of us is winning a friend of the year trophy.

"Marguerite?" Tina musters the strength to lift her head and give us both a semi-decent death stare.

"I'll ask her for her blood, and I won't let her know what it's for," Fern promises. "Just don't tell anyone that we're still together."

"I would never," I assure her.

"Ugh. Who cares about anything *you* do?" Tina's eyes drift closed.

"I think that's Tina's way of saying she won't tell anyone either," I interpret for her.

Fern nods and hurries off.

After making sure Tina is as comfortable as possible, I know there's no more putting it off.

I go to find Val.

20

Val's shift at the infirmary is just ending as I get there.

"Back again?" he asks. "I'm sure they'll be happy to see you. I heard the patients are getting a little stir crazy."

"Actually, um..." I blush and then just blurt it out. "I came to see you."

Val's eyebrows lift, along with the side of his mouth that seems to live in a semi-permanent smirk.

"I mean, if Larissa won't mind," I add in a tone that comes out snarkier than intended.

Val's smirk deepens. "No, Larissa is not the possessive type. Odd for a vampire. Usually once we know who we want, we want them to be ours and ours alone."

Val's gaze fixes on me as he says these words and is it crazy to think that he might be talking about me? But then he swivels with his usual liquid grace, calling over his shoulder, "Wait there, I need to sign off on my tests, and then we can go."

I grit my teeth, both annoyed and exhilarated to be back in Val's vortex once more. That feeling of being off-balance, hopeful, and yet totally and completely uncertain of his affections—it's disarmingly familiar.

Val comes out and slips his arm through mine, pulling me closer in the process. It's the same way we'd walk together back when we were pretend dating. Pretending in a way that began to feel way too real. I can't let those feelings for Val take over again.

I pull away, leaving a good distance between us.

He laughs softly. "Scared of getting caught doing some interspecies mingling?"

"No, I don't even care about that," I snap. "I'm more concerned about hurting Larissa's feelings."

"I already told you. She's not the jealous type."

"That doesn't mean she wants her fiancé walking arm in arm across campus with another girl." I hit the word fiancé extra hard.

Val rolls his eyes. "I hate that word. We're not engaged." My heart leaps, but then quickly settles again as he adds, "We signed a pre-marriage agreement. It's all very business-like, right down to how after two kids we can decide whether to renew the contract or go our separate ways."

"Wow," I say. The vampires definitely have their own thing going on. From talking to Greg, I've gotten the sense that shifters live pretty normal lives outside the Academy. The only weird thing Greg's ever mentioned is how his family loves to celebrate Batsgiving Day. "That's cold," I add.

"Yes, well, that's a vampire thing," Val replies dryly. He holds out a hand, inviting me to take it.

So we can hold hands? Or so I can feel his coldness?

I'm not sure. And it doesn't matter.

I reach out and grab hold.

We walk along hand in hand, his cold fingers wrapped around mine.

"Well, Larissa seems really nice at least."

"So nice," Val agrees in a way that tells me he doesn't see this as a point in her favor. "She's never set me on fire, that's for sure." He pulls us to a stop and suddenly I'm in his arms. "Edie, you set me on fire."

His eyes, dark and with depths I'll never reach, stare into mine. His cool breath fans my face as he comes closer. My eyes drift closed.

And then, at last, his lips touch mine.

The coolness of his mouth quenches the heat in mine as the kiss deepens and our tongues begin to tangle. I slide my fingers up beneath his shirt, feeling the cool carved marble that make up his abs.

I want to stand here in the sun kissing Val forever. Maybe one of the witches could make a spell to stop time. I'll have to ask Fern when she brings the blood for—

I jerk away from Val.

"Tina!"

His eyebrows rise. "No, I'm Val. We're not identical twins, so it's strange that you'd confuse us."

I slap his arm. "Val, listen. I came to get you because Tina is sick. I meant to tell you when we were alone and then got—"

But Val is already moving, a blur of boy. Then just as quickly, he is back in front of me. He grabs hold of my hands.

"Hold long has she been sick? What are the symptoms? Who knows?"

He drags me along behind him, trying to make me move at his speed, which just isn't possible.

I lean back on my heels. "Val. Hold up. Wait!"

An angry snarl is the only warning that someone else has seen us. Then, before I can even take a breath, Val's hand is ripped away from my own.

Val and Nico—in full wolf form—roll on the grass. Snarling. Cursing. Fangs flashing from both of them.

Finally, they come to a stop with Nico's paws planted on Val's chest.

"Stay away from her!" Nico barks in Val's face.

Val smiles. "Sorry, I don't speak wolf."

This earns another snarl, but Val slips out from under Nico. They face off once more, moving in a tight circle.

Pissed, I stalk over to them.

"Enough!" Fire comes out with that one word, shooting between them. With a yelp, a singed Nico leaps back. Val, meanwhile, holds out his hands like he's warming his hands at a campfire.

"Fireproof spell, remember?" he says. "See you around, Edie." He smiles and saunters off.

I know he's going to check on Tina, but I can't help feeling deserted all the same.

"Good riddance," Nico growls.

I spin on him. "Do you even know Val? Or do you just hate him because he was friends with a werewolf?"

Nico says nothing. He just glares at me with his one good eye. In werewolf form, there is no eyepatch hiding it.

I throw my hands up, totally exasperated with him. "You almost died in the desert, Nico. And I'm sure you nearly died in that prison a few times too. But now you're back here on campus, you've got a second chance at life and all you ever seem to do is treat everyone around you like shit."

He still says nothing and that unblinking glare is becoming unnerving. Still, I don't regret saying it.

"Whatever. I need to check on Cassie. You totally freaked her out with your 'kill all the monsters' routine by the way. So good job with that."

I turn my back on him. As I hurry away, his gaze nearly burns a hole between my shoulder blades.

21

Val continues sitting with Tina after I get to the room. We stay clear of talking about anything personal—including the fight he just had with Nico. Instead he politely thanks me for telling him about Tina being sick, and I fill him in on Fern's plan.

It's all sorta stilted and awkward with both of us aware that even sick, Tina would kill me if she knew about that kiss.

Finally, not wanting to draw any suspicion upon Tina, Val leaves to go about his normal routine. I promise to let him know if Tina's condition changes.

That night, in her delirium, Tina tells me more than she ever would if she were well.

"My father, the hypocrite, always told us that being pure-blood vampire was important. That we could never, under any circumstances, let anyone know the truth."

"What is the truth?" I ask gently.

She laughs weakly. "The truth is that our mother was a mutt. A bit of shifter, a bit of nymph, a bit of vampire. She had no pedigree. No connections. But she was very beautiful. My father took her into his household as a pet. He dressed her up like a doll and showed her off at parties and well, things became complicated."

"When she got pregnant my father's wife wanted her dead. But father had no children yet, so he convinced her to wait until she gave birth. Maybe he loved my mother. Maybe not. But when Val and I were born, he looked the other way when his wife murdered our mother and took us as her own.

"I think my father's wife does love us in her own way. We call her Mother, but she doesn't understand us. She wants us to be just like her. But we're not. Even when we were children, nothing was ever good enough—especially when our other characteristics would show."

"Like you turning your hair green," I muse.

"And I talked to plants, like, all the time," Tina says. She clucks her tongue at Vee, who turns its trap...what I've come to think of as its head, toward Tina. "If they were thirsty they would tell me, and I'd...."

Tina blinks, as if suddenly remembering who I am. She tells me to bring her water. But it's too cold. Then too warm. I go back and forth at least six times and then she takes one sip and says she's not thirsty anymore.

Ordering me around seems to put her back in a better mood, though, because as she leans back against her pillows (and actually mine too—she demanded it and when I objected said that it would be too bad if borrowing my pillow turned out to be her dying wish), she continues her story.

"So, my father made sure we learned how to be perfect vampires. They wanted to fool everyone. They wanted to fool themselves most of all, I think. When we were young they tried to keep our birth mom a secret, but I always knew we were different. 'Mother' told me the truth when I was five years old. She told me I could tell no one and that I needed to keep my 'Moggy' side a secret. It was easier for me, but Val..."

"Val what...?" I prompt.

"Oh, Val. We're twins but I've always felt older. Always felt like it was my job to protect him. I know you like him, and he likes you, but I can't let anything seem off about him. You understand, don't you? He's the only thing I care about."

She goes silent again and I can't help but feel for her. Not knowing your birth mother, I understand. I feel a kinship with Tina, something I thought wasn't possible.

Fern returns with the blood; there's got to be at least a gallon and all I can think is that Marguerite must really love her. She sets up an IV drip and tells Tina that we'll be back to check on her after our next class.

"Next class?" I ask Fern, confused.

"Well, you know how I was talking to Hermes about how disappointed we all were that sex-ed was cancelled because Zee wanted Mad Maddox instead?"

"Yeah, you really saved our butts."

"Well, I may have been a little *too* convincing. He petitioned Zee and now we have two special guest speakers."

"No. Please no."

She gives me a half grin. "Yep. Old man Priapus is on campus now."

"Are you sure?" I ask, hurrying to keep up.

"He's kind of hard to miss," she says, turning to me with a smile. I can see it's supposed to be a joke, and she can tell I'm not getting it.

"You don't know who Priapus is, do you?" she asks, hand on the classroom door.

I shake my head.

"Don't worry," she says, with something of a smirk. "All will soon be made clear."

———

Its not only made clear. It's made abundantly, enormously, engorgedly, obvious.

Priapus stands at the front of the classroom, hands on his hips, toga draped over one shoulder, watching students file in. Normal teacher behavior, except for the fact that his toga is open at the hips and his ridiculously large dick rests inside a wheelbarrow in front of him. I mean, it's covered with what looks like a giant tube sock, but he definitely doesn't have an extra foot in that wheelbarrow. It's a dick in a sock.

"Uh..." I've lost verbal abilities. There are no words for this.

Suddenly, Cassie is at my side. She takes me by the elbow and guides me over to where Fern and Larissa are sitting.

"God of fertility," Cassie informs me, in a low whisper. "Protector of gardens, fruit plants, and livestock."

"Okay," I say. "The fertility part makes sense, but protector of—"

Cassie smacks herself on the forehead. "Also, male genitals," she adds. "I forgot that part. Protector of male genitals."

"There it is," I say. Everything makes sense now.

I settle in next to Fern, who also leans in to educate me.

"Apparently a long time ago he used to use it as a counterweight on the scales," she says.

"I..." Nope. Lost all words again.

Nico comes sauntering in late. He drops into the seat at

the edge of our row, right next to Cassie. Unbelievable! When his werewolf-as-Rambo impression left her nearly catatonic. I lean over with the intention of telling him to get lost, but Cassie gets there first.

"Nico." She takes his hand in both of hers. "I meant to tell you, thank you so much for coming back for me."

My mouth almost drops open.

Nico gives a half shrug. "You helped me escape." He hesitates and then in a voice so soft I can barely hear it over the classroom chatter, he adds, "You helped me survive in that place."

Cassie leans even further into him; she's practically nuzzling his shoulder. "I knew you'd come back." Pulling back from him, Cassie frowns. "But you promised you wouldn't kill anyone."

"I promised I wouldn't kill anyone when I was escaping," Nico corrects. "And I didn't."

Cassie looks so sad at this. Her eyes fill with tears. I watch Nico watching her. He swallows and looks away.

But Cassie isn't done with him. "You have a good heart, Nico," she says softly. "I saw you be kind. I know it's in you."

Nico doesn't answer and before Cassie can say anything else, he's saved by the start of class.

"Class, everyone settle down," Priapus says, holding his hands up for quiet. "I don't want to have to say it twice. I don't want to get hard on you."

There's a titter of giggles, but apparently Priapus didn't mean it as a joke, because his eyebrows come together.

"Alright, everyone," he says. "Welcome to Comprehensive Sexual Education for Non-Humans. I am your teacher, Priapus, but you can all me Pus."

There's some nervous laughter, but apparently that wasn't a joke either because his face gets stormier.

"All right, get all the giggles out. Every time I teach this class, I hope the students will have evolved and be able to handle a frank discussion of sexuality." He sighs heavily. "But it hasn't happened yet. And yet I press on, determined to ram this information into your heads. It might be uncomfortable at first, but if everyone would just relax, I believe this could be a pleasurable experience for all of us."

Oh my gods! Can he hear himself?

Priapus grabs his wheelbarrow and wheels over to the whiteboard, dick leading the way. "Now, let us begin with the difference between boys and girls."

We all glance at each other. Is he serious?

"Now," Priapus says. "Boys have a pee-pee."

He draws a cock and balls on the whiteboard complete with a smattering of hair, then turns his wheelbarrow again so he's facing us.

"Can you say it with me, class?"

Okay, he is serious.

"Pee pee," everyone repeats, which seems to please him.

Cassie's face is beet red and I think she's about to fall over from lack of oxygen. Fern has her arms crossed in front of her, apparently insulted as a healer. Val leans back in his chair, arms above his head. His coolly amused attitude is not all that different from how he is in every class. And Larissa...

Larissa is taking notes. She's drawn a huge cock and balls and written "pee-pee" next to it, in big, curlicue lettering.

I am heartbroken for Jordan. He will be crushed when he finds out what he missed.

"Um, Mister uh... Mister Pus?" A merman has his hand in the air, a question on his face.

"Yes?" Priapus asks.

"We're uh... I mean, we kind of already know the basics,"

he says. "I think Mr. Zee wanted you to concentrate more on why interspecies breeding is a bad idea."

"It *is* a bad idea," Priapus says. A few heads nod in agreement. "But I don't think you *do* know your basics, son."

"I—" the merman begins, but Priapus cuts him off.

"What is the name for female genitalia?"

"It's, uh..." he reddens a bit, looking around. "It's a vagina, sir."

"Wrong!" Priapus holds his finger up in the air. "The female genitalia is called a *hoo-hoo*."

And with that, Priapus draws a very accurate rendition of a vagina, carefully labeling it "hoo-hoo."

Nico stands. "Yeah, that's enough for me. I'm done." Without another word he turns and walks out of the classroom.

Priapus shakes a finger at Nico's retreating back, "That young man has his head up his pooper."

"I could literally be saving lives right now," Fern says, arms still crossed.

Larissa, hurriedly scribbling in her notebook, gives us a huge smile.

"I had no idea you had different names for them here!" she says. "America is fascinating!"

22

After class, Themis meets me in the hall and asks me to follow her. I want to check on Tina, but I can't exactly use that as an excuse.

"Edie," she says once we're in her office. "This is for you." She hands me pair of portal keys.

"What is this for?" I ask thoroughly confused.

"Those will get you to Greece and back. To find your mom."

This is the day for me losing all control of my vocal cords. Apparently also my eyes. They're filling up with tears, and I don't know how to thank Themis.

"I know that there's no way Zee will send you now," Themis says. "Not with Maddox running the show. All missions are approved by her and your mom isn't a priority. Maddox is more interested in killing than rescue missions."

"You don't agree with her view, do you?" I ask, relieved that Themis hasn't caught Maddox fever.

"No. I don't. But many here do." She hands me a school pack. "There is some food, some money, and as long as you're wearing this, you can speak and understand modern

Greek. There's also your old cell phone. I spelled the GPS to bring you to your mother."

I hug her, but she's rigid as a board.

"I can't thank you enough."

She gives me a squeeze—one that feels a little more like being crushed due to her amazing strength—and then releases me.

"I'm not doing this just for you," she says. "Your mother and I...we were close once. I raised your dad as my own, and mothers are protective of their sons. She had to win her way into my heart after she claimed his. No easy task." She raises an eyebrow at me.

"I bet not."

Themis clears her throat, back to business.

"You have to go alone," she tells me. "And I don't think you should bring your mom back with you. I understand you need to see she is unscathed. However, she's safe where she is now. Safe from the monsters and safe from...well, from here."

"There are no monsters with my mom? Did you get new intel?"

She shakes her head curtly. "I have my own sources. I don't know everything, but...please, Edie, let your mom know that you are well and return to us. We need you."

I turn to leave but she stops me. "Tell her I miss her. And that I am sorry about your dad. Tell her...tell her I will watch out for you as best I can."

"I will," I promise.

I make my way to the portal, determined not to get waylaid.

In the distance, I catch sight of Nico and Maddox. They have a crowd gathered around them, most of them chanting something about monster blood making the grass grow.

Several feet away Cassie stands alone, wearing a clearly homemade sandwich board and banging a drum with each word as she counter-protests, "End the war! Live in peace!"

I feel like I should join her. She looks so alone. But at the same time I don't know if I believe in her message any more than I do Maddox's.

Pretending not to see any of them, I turn my head and hurry to the portal.

At least all the protesting is a good distraction.

I won't have any tag-alongs or team members. I'm going in alone this time, and it feels like maybe that's the way it should've been from the start.

I throw the portal key into the fountain and step through the glowing space between the pillars. Into the freezing nothingness. When I take the next step, I am on a bustling city street.

Finally—Greece.

———

I immediately pull out my phone and open the maps app. I'm in Athens.

Last year I was devastated when I realized I wasn't going with my family to Greece. What would have happened if I hadn't gotten sick? Would my dad be alive? Or would we *all* be dead?

I shake my head. I can't play the 'what if' game right now. I have to find my mom. Who is apparently on a small island off the coast.

I hail a cab and tell him to take me to somewhere I can rent a boat.

I want to be alone with my thoughts, so of course the cabbie tries to make small talk.

"American?" he asks.

"Yes...on a school trip," I say, realizing I forgot to have my uniform spelled to street clothes.

"How long are you in Athens?"

"Not long. I'm taking a side trip. We were given the day to explore."

"You speak very good Greek," he tells me approvingly. "Are your parents from here?"

I start to say no, but then I realize I have no idea where my bio parents were born. My mother's name is Greek so she could be from here—she could even be from Athens. I shake my head and answer with shrug.

"I just picked up the language easily," I tell him. I don't add from a magical spell.

At the docks I shove money at the cabbie and I guess it was a lot because he thanks me profusely. Finding a boat is harder than finding a cab. A lot of the fishermen ignore me, while others seem super sketchy. One shouts, "I'll give you a ride, pretty girl."

I realize that with the time difference it's almost dark. Who needs a boat? As soon as the sun sets I'll just fly.

I walk along the beach until I find a less populated area. Settling on the sand, I watch the setting sun. It's so beautiful but I can't enjoy it. I'm about to see my mom, and I have no idea what it's going to be like. Joyful, obviously. But, to what extent? Does she even know Dad is dead? Am I going to have to tell her? And what happened to Mavis? Themis obviously knew something, and she didn't send me after Mavis—just Mom. Somehow the two got separated, and having to tell me all about it is certainly going to be painful.

Especially if Mavis is dead.

"No," I say out loud. "She's not. She can't be."

When it's finally dark enough to shift into my dragon

form, I jump into the air and spread my wings, flying higher and higher. The warm air is lovely. I head toward the island where my mom is waiting.

When I get there I circle a few times. There's a tiny village and a lighthouse. I land on the far side of the island and make my way up a cliffside path. Checking my phone, I walk straight to the lighthouse and the small cottage that connects to it. When I get to the door I pause. According to the information on my phone—this is it.

With a shaking hand, I knock.

I hear voices inside. A deep one and several high-pitched ones. A boy opens the door, he's only about eight or nine. When he sees me his face scrunches in confusion. "Who are you?"

"Kostas, don't be rude," a familiar voice says and suddenly she's there. My mother stands next to the boy, a hand on his shoulder.

"Yes?" she asks. She looks at me expectantly and I burst into tears.

"Oh dear, come in, come in." She hustles me inside.

"Who is this?" a burly man with a beard asks.

"I don't know. She was at the door. Maybe she's lost?" My mom guides me toward a kitchen table and gestures for me to sit.

"How do all these lost women wash up on our island?" he asks with a smile on his lips. He leans in close to me. "You, did you fall in the water? Do you know who you are? Do you know your name?"

"Edie," I whisper. My mother gives me a strange look, then shakes her head.

"Well. Let's get Edie some tea, maybe add some sambuca?" she tells the man and he nods and goes to the kitchen.

Mom gives me a nervous glance, then a weird, polite, smile. A smile you use on a stranger.

"Don't you know me?" I ask, my voice cracking as tears start to form.

"No, honey. Are you lost?"

I shake my head. "I'm not lost. I thought *you* were."

She kneels next to me. "Do you know *me*?" she asks quietly.

Before I can answer a cry comes from another room. My mother hustles away and comes back carrying a baby. She coos at it and smiles.

"She's only one month old," she tells me, showing off her baby girl. "My pride and joy!"

The world falls out from under me.

I open my mouth to tell her she's my mother too, but the words won't come out.

Instead, I hear myself say, "I heard there was a woman with amnesia living here."

"I hate that word," she says. "Amnesia. So silly." She makes a face and shakes her head. It's such a familiar expression of hers. When we say something silly or that she finds absurd.

My whole chest squeezes with pain.

My mother sits next to me, the baby on her shoulder.

"But yes, that is apparently the proper term. I washed up on shore over a year ago. Kostas found me and his father took me in. I had no memory of who I was but...well, one thing led to another."

"Did you try to find out who you were?" I ask. "Before you had some random guy's baby?"

She doesn't catch the mix of fury and despair in my voice. Or maybe she just doesn't want to.

"Of course, I tried for months. But, no luck. Finally, I

decided. Enough. I like it here. I'm happy. I don't need to remember my other life to know this is where I belong."

The man—my mother's new husband—sets a mug of tea in front of me and I sip it. It's hot and tastes of licorice.

"Do you know my wife?" he asks. "Do you know who she is?"

They all stare at me expectantly, even the little boy. I down my tea and get to my feet.

"No, I was just out walking and got a little lost. My family has a boat. I should get back to them before they worry."

"Yes, of course," my mother smiles. "Do you want Kostas to guide you? He knows every inch of this island!" She beams at him proudly and the little boy blushes.

"No, I'm good. Thank you for the tea and for…"

I stop. I have no idea what to say.

"Good-bye."

I flee, waving a hand over my shoulder, desperately needing to get away from the house. I run all the way back to the beach before I once again burst into tears.

I sit in the sand, not caring when the tide comes in and soaks me. I'm just about ready to leave when a voice behind me calls my name.

"Edie…?"

I turn and almost fall into the water.

Standing before me on the beach is my sister, Mavis.

23

It's a trick, I know. A monster—maybe a selkie—sent in my sister's skin to confuse me. As soon as I go to her, I'll be pulled under the waves and drowned.

I don't care. I'm willing to take the chance.

I rush into her arms and suddenly we're both crying, her hands going up and down my back as she assesses the new Edie—taller, stronger—and I take in her familiar scent, something I've never been able to pin down. Fur and old books, maybe. It's so particular to Mavis that I know it's my sister, not some imposter, and my tears start fresh.

Mavis is alive.

She leads me away from the beach to a cliffside cave where there's a sleeping bag and supplies.

I wipe my face. "Is this where you've been the entire time?"

"No," she shakes her head. "It's a long story."

We sit on the sleeping bag and she pulls a cooking pot out of a pile to heat up some canned soup. It's not until she passes me a bowl of the steaming mixture, I realize how hungry I am. I gulp it down, then start to cry again, my face a wet soggy mess.

"I found Mom." I start. "She didn't know who I was."

"I know," Mavis tells me, wiping my face with a towel.

I hiccup. "And she's not our bio mom."

"I know that too," she tells me softly.

"And the Greek gods are real and also I'm a dragon."

"A dragon?" Mavis barks out a laugh. "Seriously? Wow, Edie. You certainly beat me out in that arena. I'm a freaking housecat."

Wait. What? I swallow and really look at my sister, her face suddenly new and different to me in the firelight.

"You're a shifter too?"

I'm realizing as little as I knew about my parents, I might have known even less about my sister. Resentment rises up in my chest, but I push it down.

Mavis, *my Mavis*, is sitting in front of me.

I want to crumble then. I want her to stroke my hair and tell me it'll be okay. But that was never Mavis' style—that was all Mom. A Mom who wasn't actually my mom and doesn't remember me now.

"Mavis, please, tell me what happened. How you're involved in all this. I need to understand."

She turns to fiddle with the fire before answering and I wonder if she's as scared as me.

Such a thought would never have occurred to me before. I'd always believed Mavis could fix anything, beat anyone, and look good doing it.

But right now, my sister looks unsure. Maybe even scared.

"I never went away to college," she tells me at last. "I went to Mount Olympus Academy instead."

"Why didn't you tell me?"

"Dad said you were too young. He was keeping us safe."

"Dad would never tell you and not me!" The words burst out of me, unchecked.

Mom and Mavis were always out running around, doing their own thing, while Dad sat with me at home, signing off piles on detentions, while I sucked on my inhaler.

"Edie, he was going to tell you when you were eighteen." Mavis uses her calm big sister tone that always set my teeth on edge. "Dad wanted us to have a normal life right up until we were ready for the adult world."

"Or the magical world," I add, shaking my head. "So it's our call? Go to college and become an engineer or go to the Academy and become a dragon? What sort of choice is that? If our parents—if you—were honest with me, maybe things wouldn't have turned out so shitty."

"Edie!" There's a clear reprimand in her voice. "Hear me out before you start spouting off as usual. There's a lot I need to tell you, and I need to know you can handle it."

"Seriously?" Sniffing, I scrub my sleeve across my runny nose. "Do you always have to do the big sister thing?" Yesterday I would have begged to have Mavis 'big sister' me. Now...it feels like she's patronizing me.

Reaching into her supply bag she hands me a travel pick of tissues. I snatch it away before she can hold one to my nose and tell me to blow.

"Edie, I *am* your big sister."

"What does that even mean anymore? I'm not the sickly little girl you left behind. I've survived losing dad, I thought I lost you too. I've fought. I've," I pause but continue, "I've killed."

"Oh Edie," she says, softly. Pitying.

She's using her big sister voice. The one that always sets my teeth on edge. The one that clearly communicates, we are not peers—you are my underling. I can't even count how many fights started with Mavis using that tone. But there's also sympathy in Mavis' face. Fire roils in my belly, wanting to melt it away. The joyful reunion I dreamed of having with my sister is going up in smoke.

I thought if I could just get my family back, everything would be okay. But it's not. Mavis is not going to swoop in and save the day. And I don't want her to. I've learned how to save myself.

But that doesn't mean I'm not angry.

Angry at Dad for trusting Mavis with the secret and not me.

Angry at Mom for not knowing who I am after everything I've been through to find her.

Angry at Mavis for being so calm and collected, even when everything I thought was true has been turned upside down—again.

And I can already tell the internal earthquakes aren't ending anytime soon.

Why can't any piece of my life stay locked down in the same place?

After a year of wanting to speak with Mavis, now I don't want to hear what she has to say.

But I have to. Dad isn't going to wander into this cave and demand to know what we're bickering about now. Mom isn't going to make her cheesy, "Oh, I thought it was World War III, but it's just you girls fighting again," joke.

I let out a shuddering breath. "Fine. Continue."

Mavis frowns slightly. As if she hadn't expected that response. Or as if she'd wanted to goad me into a fight.

Maybe this conversation is as difficult for her as it is for me.

"I learned a lot when I came to the Academy," Mavis

says. "Some of it was exactly what I expected, but there were other things...things that didn't quite fit. I started asking questions. And..." She takes a deep breath before continuing. "As a housecat, it's quite easy to eavesdrop. I overheard a lot of things not meant for my ears."

Of course she did. That's Mavis. Nancy Drew, complete with a fluffy tail.

"I heard things that contradicted what I'd been taught. I heard things that made me realize I had to do something. I had to help them."

"Help who?" I ask.

"The monsters."

"What?!" I shoot to my feet, my head spinning, the food in my stomach flash-frying a second time as a burst of fire wells up inside me. She couldn't have said—but she did. Mavis was helping the monsters.

"Edie," Mavis says softly, looking up at me, is that a hint of fear in her eyes? "Most of the time I was at the Academy I was working for the monsters. I used what I learned in spy class for them—as a double agent. Ocypete was my contact and my code name was...Emmie."

"Emmie?!"

Oh. My. Gods.

I stumble back. I can't help it; I have to release some of my rage. My wings pop out, a bright fire red. Flame shoots from my mouth.

"You're the traitor," I gasp. "You..." My brain whirls. "You tried to kill Nico! He was tortured in a monster prison because of you!"

"Nico?" She comes toward me. I hold a hand out. A warning to keep her distance. "He's *alive*? How do you know him?"

I laugh, but the sound is bitter. "No, you wanted to finish telling your story first. Remember?"

Mavis shakes her head. "I know how hard this must be for you."

"You have no idea! You never did. I was always your sickly little sister sitting home with an inhaler and a bad back, while you were out in the big bright world getting ready to conquer it." I take a step toward her now. But not with a hand out. "Did you conquer it, Mavis? Or should I say, Emmie?" The hot bile rises in my throat.

Mavis gives a small shake of her head. "I think it's safe to say that the world conquered me. I mean, look at me." She throws out her arms, showing off the cavern around her. "I'm living in a freaking cave. Eating canned soup for every meal. Our mother lives up the road with her new happy family and puts out a can of tuna each night because she thinks I'm a nice stray cat. That's the highlight of my days. Mom, petting my head, telling me I'm a nice kitty."

Suddenly all the anger goes out of me. "Oh. Mavis, I'm so... Sorry. I am. About everything. Mom and Dad and Grandma..."

We are in each other's arms then, sobbing. Mourning the loss of not just Mom, but Dad and Grandma and every mundane thing in our old lives that we never fully appreciated until it was gone.

At last, we pull apart and wipe our faces.

"Who did that to her?" I ask. "Who took Mom's memories?"

"The monsters...there's a cockatrice that can manipulate memories. It's not true they kill with a look. But they can erase a person's 'past life.' So in essence they take their life."

"See! The monsters *are* bad." I can't believe she can't see it too.

"No, you're not understanding. They erased her memory for a good reason."

"And what was their reason?" I ask, my voice near to yelling.

"Mom asked them to," she tells me. "She wanted all of her memories taken away."

24

I gape at her. Too shocked to be upset. "She would never."

"Oh, Edie, you don't know what she was like after Levi killed Dad..."

"Levi, *the monster*," I stress. How can she be so blind?

"It's not that simple. Look, losing Dad was bad enough, but when my contacts in the resistance told us you were dead, Mom lost her shit. She could barely function. I didn't know someone could cry so much. But the worst part was when she stopped crying. It was so bad, Edie. It was almost like she was a different person. Like something had permanently broken inside of her. She was scared all the time, certain they were going to kill us too." A tear slides down Mavis' face.

Tucking away her tissue, Mavis continues, "I thought she'd get past it. Go back to being Mom. But she only got worse. She started drinking. She said it made her feel light again. It let her forget." Mavis sighs. "Mom begged me to help her find someone to cast the memory spell. I said to her, 'Mom, you'll forget me too' and she said... 'Look at me.

What sort of mother am I to you anymore? I'm holding you back.' I told her it wasn't true. I told her...I don't even know. Anything I could think of to make her feel better. But it wasn't enough. The next day she slipped away when my back was turned. A few days later the cockatrice returned her. She had no idea who I was."

Mavis is crying softly and I want to tell her that it's okay. That Mom doing this wasn't her fault. But I'm too twisted up inside. I have no idea what was anybody's fault.

I reach for Mavis and hug her as tight as I can.

In the year we've been apart, I've gotten taller and stronger. Size-wise, she's now the littler sister.

We don't say much more after that. I think we both feel too heavy to get anymore words out. Technically, she's my enemy now. But she was my sister first.

We pass out on her sleeping bag. I sleep dreamlessly and wake to Mavis making tea. We sip our hot drinks in silence.

"C'mon," Mavis says at last, holding a hand out to me. "Let's go for a walk."

I take it and she leads me out of the cave, onto the beach where the sun is rising.

The waves lick our toes. Despite my heartache I try to admire the beauty of Mom's new home.

Matter-of-factly, Mavis begins to tell me the story of her spy days.

"Working for the monsters started off as small things. Giving Ocypete a head's up about missions, so she could get that info out to her contacts. Trying to mitigate the death toll and yes, even sabotage."

I can't hold back a groan. Sabotage for gods' sake! It's even worse than I thought.

"But then I was tasked with recruitment," Mavis continues. "Getting more Academy students on our side. Opening their eyes to the unfairness and hypocrisy of the gods. Jenn LaMont was easy to turn. She hated the rigidness of vampire society. And there was a bat shifter, and a witch..."

"Fern," I say quietly.

Mavis looks at me, surprised. "You know them?"

"I do attend the Academy now. Fern is my friend."

"And the others?" she asks. "I picked them because they weren't popular or flashy. They didn't stick out."

"The rest are dead."

She looks like she's been struck.

"Ocypete killed them..." I say, realizing that it makes no sense. Why would Pity kill them if they were working for her?

Why haven't I thought this out before?

The answer is obvious—because I didn't want to.

"She would never," Mavis says. "Pity would die for any of her informants."

I don't say anything. How long has Mavis been in this cave? Does she even know that Ocypete is dead?

Looking agitated, Mavis continues, "I used to go on a lot of missions with Nico. We were good together. He really liked me. I liked him too, when he wasn't being a bossy dick-head. But I was also falling for Derrick, another werewolf. I knew that I would never be able to recruit Nico to the cause, but Derrick, he was different. He even had a vampire room-mate; the guy was a typical vampire jerk, but he and Derrick were friends. It was weird and sweet. Like one of those bromance buddy movies."

"It sounds crazy, but I kinda loved both of them," she tells me. "But I couldn't let Nico know. He hated Derrick; I guess maybe he could tell I had a thing for him. It's hard to hide, sometimes." She smiles, sadly.

"I meant to break things off with Nico, tell him we

couldn't be partners anymore. It was too dangerous; I knew he'd go berserk if he ever guessed I was a monster informant. I just needed to get through one more mission with him. After that I planned on asking to be reassigned with Derrick. Nico and I were on that last mission together when I got news about your pneumonia. I asked him to cover for me and came home to see you. Once I was back, I was so sick of all the spying and the lies... I just wanted to be normal again."

Her eyes are on the sunrise as she continues. "I was tired, and confused, and sick of constantly being in danger. I came home and told Dad I'd made my choice. I wanted the real world. I wanted to get a job in Greece, and to get away from the Academy altogether. But Nico caught up to me."

"And?" I ask, as Mavis pauses.

"Nico did more than cover for me. He followed me home. He's one of the Academy's best spies—it was easy for him to eavesdrop on my conversations with Dad. He knew everything. My feelings for the monsters, Derrick, and even him. When he showed up on the airplane, I was terrified. I knew he'd never let me go without a fight. I messaged Dad, told him that Nico had tracked me down. But he didn't have his phone on, so I could only hope he could get an ally to the airport in time when we landed. Someone who could help me..."

Mavis looks scared, just remembering. "I couldn't get hold of Dad, and the flight attendants were telling everyone to turn off their phones. So, I sent you a selfie of me with him, right before takeoff."

"Wait, that was...Nico?"

"I figured if the worst happened. If... if he killed me, then at least when you turned eighteen and Dad told you everything...if you chose to go to the Academy. Maybe you would recognize him. Maybe you would figure out this was your sister's murderer."

I think of that selfie, two beautiful people smiling for the camera. Two people intent on killing one another in order to survive.

"You severely disfigured him," I remind her. The boy I found wandering, naked and beaten in the desert, looked nothing like the suave guy in that picture.

"There wasn't any help for it," Mavis says. "I didn't want to hurt him, but... oh, Edie." She shivers. "He was so angry."

I can't help but shudder, too. I've seen Nico when he's mad. I wouldn't want that directed at me.

"And so?"

"So I hurt him. Badly."

"I'd say," I snort. "He's missing an eye."

She laughs in that new dry way she has. "Yes, there. But also...emotionally. The way he was raised, he's so stunted. I think my rejection of him hurt worse than the knife in his eye.

"Anyway, I went back to the Academy. I couldn't stand the idea of recovery missions being sent out to find Nico, putting my classmates in danger. I thought I'd killed him, so I pinned that on a monster. Told them our mission had failed and Nico was lost."

"Going back to the Academy that first day, walking through the swamp to the gate, I was so afraid. I didn't know if Nico had blown my cover but I had to get Derrick out. We'd talked about leaving for good, escaping together, just letting the gods and monsters fight it out without us. And for a while, it worked! I returned a hero."

"Then what happened?" I ask. "Why didn't you just leave?"

"We were going to. But first I had to warn my recruits.

Which took some time, because I didn't want to draw attention to them or their relationship with me." She pauses and look at me. "If they're all dead, I must've screwed that up." Mavis shakes her head. "I did everything wrong and somewhere along the way a healer who spies for Themis caught me and Derrick in our secret rendezvous spot. We tried to play it off like we were in the midst of some hot and heavy petting. But she didn't buy it. I barely escaped with my life. Derrick was not so lucky. That's when I decided to devote my whole life to the cause. I'm lucky they were still willing to take me after I'd messed up so many times."

Gods. It's suddenly clear that guilt is eating Mavis alive. She's taken responsibility for every bad thing that's happened in the last year. It's so typical Mavis. Annoying how she believes her actions affect everyone and everything. But also amazing that she cares so much and never ever gives up.

"It's going to be alright," I tell her, suddenly the big sister in the situation.

"It is," she nods, lifting her chin up. "But we need *you*, Edie. You're in the perfect position to take over my work at the Academy."

"No. I'm not."

"But I can't do it. I'm burned. Why do you think I'm living on this island, out of the way? I can't spy anymore. I'm on the gods' most wanted list. There's a spell on this island that keeps me—and Mom—out of the gods' line of sight."

"I'm not switching sides," I tell her. I think of Fern, how she was with the monsters for a while. How persuasive Ocypete was. I see how Mavis got caught up with them.

"But..." She looks desperate now. How did Mavis allow herself to be taken advantage of like this?

I want to help her, she's so obviously lost. But at the

same time she has to know—I will never join her against the Academy.

"Do you know that Ocypete brought the monsters to the Academy and killed people?" I ask, the fire in my gut returning. "That your mentor killed my friends?"

Mavis' eyes widen. "That's not... Ocypete doesn't want students harmed. Only the gods."

"You don't know, do you? Ocypete is dead."

She shakes her head. "No..."

"Do you want to know how she died?"

Mavis—the sister that I wanted to see for so long—looks at me with horror in her eyes as I reveal the person I have become.

"I killed her."

25

Mavis turns her back to me. The sun is bright now, and I have to shade my eyes as she walks away, head down, obviously crying.

I don't know how I feel. My sister, the person I've looked up to my whole life, actively helped the monsters who raided the Spring Fling and killed Darcy. She almost killed Nico. She made the decision—without me—to help Mom erase her memories.

Mavis turns back, walking toward me like each foot weighs a thousand pounds. When she's up close she reaches out, takes both my hands, looks me in the eye and says, "I forgive you."

"You forgive *me*?" I shriek. I've listened to Mavis' shit all last night and then again this morning, but this is the final straw. "For what? For defending the Academy? For helping my friends? What about you, Mavis? Don't you need forgiveness?"

She shakes her head, hair blowing in the breeze. "I don't forgive me. How could I ask it of you?"

This knocks me back a step.

But then I hear the screams of the dying from the Spring Fling. Sometimes the sound still wakes me in the middle of the night. I feel horrible that Mavis is so obviously broken in ways not obvious on the outside, but I also really need her to acknowledge how bad Ocypete really was.

"And what about your mentor, Pity? She led the monsters who decapitated a merman for no reason other than he was standing in the way."

Mavis' eyebrows draw together, confused.

"And kidnapped a seer who may never recover from the shock."

Her mouth opens, but nothing comes out.

"And tortured a werewolf who was already half-dead—"

"The monsters wouldn't do those things," Mavis says, interrupting me. "Ocypete was always very clear—no harm to students. Ever. That was the golden rule."

"Ha! Well, it was broken the second Darcy's head hit the floor."

"Wait," Mavis grabs my arm. "Did Ocypete give that order?"

"What? No." I shake her off, irritated that she's stuck on details. "But she couldn't control her soldiers and a minotaur—"

"Falcus," Mavis says, her tone suddenly hard. "Gods damn it."

"What?" I ask again. Now it's my turn to be confused.

A family shows up on the beach, the mom and older child running ahead, the younger one struggling in deep sand, the father holding her arms for balance. We both watch for a second, remembering when that was our family.

"Come on," Mavis leads me away, dropping her voice. "Falcus was always a loose cannon. He didn't think Ocypete took enough risks, or was hard enough to do the difficult things. She always said that the students were only human shields, but Falcus argued that you've got to smash the shield to get to the god standing behind it."

It's a terrible thought, but accurate. I'd seen more than a few students smashed that night. And yet not one god lifted even a finger against the monsters attacking us.

"Edie," she goes on. "I think Falcus may have splintered off from the main group, the monsters I worked for. With Ocypete dead..." She swallows hard, clears her throat. "With Ocypete dead, there would have been no strong leadership among the monsters who were only fighting for what they believed they deserved—freedom from the gods."

"Oh, the kinder, gentler monsters," I scoff.

"Yes," Mavis squeezes my wrist. "Falcus must have talked other malcontents into coming over to his point of view. Torturing Nico, kidnapping a seer..." Mavis shakes her head. "That's not something the monsters I know would do."

"Really?" I ask, snapping my hand away. "And what about Leviathan, huh? How well do you know him, Mavis? Because he killed our dad!"

"Levi..." Mavis pushes some hair out of her eyes. "Well, that's complicated."

I cross my arms and stare her down. From behind us comes the sounds of the family, happily playing in the surf.

"Themis hinted at that," I say. "She said something about Dad and Levi having a history. But I'm guessing it's not written down anywhere, and I'm not leaving this beach until I know."

"Okay, okay," Mavis sighs, sits down on a piece of driftwood and pats the spot beside her, inviting me to sit. I don't want to sit. I want to sprout wings and fly and maybe burn half of Greece. But there's a nice family not too far from me, and I've already killed enough.

I sit.

"Gods and monsters aren't all that different from us," Mavis says. "They have enemies and old feuds and...and they fall in love."

"Sure." In the mythology book I've been reading gods were always falling in and out of love.

"And sometimes they fall in love with humans," she says, holding my gaze. "And when that love isn't returned, just like us, they're hurt. And sometimes they get angry. Sometimes, people die."

"What does that have to do with Levi and Dad?"

Oh...wait. Tears are forming in Mavis' eyes, threatening to spill over.

The tide crashes up to our feet, soaking them in cold seawater. Cold like the spray that hit me that day when Levi came for our father

"Are you saying that Levi was in love with Mom?" I ask, incredulous.

"Deeply," Mavis nods. "Mom and Dad tried to reach a hand out to the monsters. They hoped to see some sort of peace settlement between the gods and monsters one day, but..." She sighs, looking out over the water. "Love makes things complicated."

I want to have a smartass comeback for that, but I don't. I don't because it's true. Love does make things complicated —look at Mavis coming back for Derrick after stabbing Nico, uncertain if she was returning to certain death.

Look at Tina making every effort to cover for Val and ensure everyone believes he's a full-blooded vampire.

And Val...Val's mouth on mine, neither one of us remembering that he's engaged.

I shake my head. I can't think about that right now.

"Levi had been checking in on Mom, surreptitiously, for

a long time," Mavis says. "When we went to Greece and Dad stayed behind, he hoped that our parents were separated. He found us, came on strong. Mom rejected him, in no uncertain terms. And I was right beside her—telling him to take his fish stank out of our faces."

"Oh, Mavis," I say, sadly, realizing this was yet one more thing for Mom to hold against her.

"And that made Levi really mad, so he took his fish stank to our side of the Atlantic."

Tears fill Mavis' eyes. "Mom says I tipped him over the edge. That I should've let her handle it."

"He was a crazy monster. You can't blame yourself for how he reacted."

Mavis shrugs in response, clearly not buying this.

"But wait," I say. "What about Grandma? She died in the elevator, not on the beach. And why would Levi want to hurt her?"

"I don't think he did," Mavis says carefully, guarding her words. "I don't know who killed Grandma, Edie," she says. "But I can tell you this—I'm pretty sure someone else was there that day."

26

I'm exhausted. Mentally and physically.

I've learned so much from Mavis, but what now? Make a home with her on this island? We couldn't even share a room back home, so it's probably not a great idea for both of us to squeeze into this little cave and pine after a mom who will never remember us. And, unlike Mavis, I couldn't exactly visit her in dragon form every evening. I don't think I could get away with that!

"I'm going back to the Academy," I tell Mavis. "If I stay away much longer, I'll be missed."

"How did you get away?"

"Themis snuck me a key."

"Don't trust Themis," she said, shifting once more into bossy big sister mode. "She's all for the Academy. If it came down to protecting you or protecting the school, she's Mount Olympus all the way."

"You're the second person to tell me that this week," I say. "Nico was the other."

Her eyes widen. "Well, it doesn't make less true."

"Maybe not, but here's a truth you probably don't know.

Themis is on the outs with Mr. Zee right now, so her giving
me the key was a risk. And, despite outward appearances,
she's not an emotionless robot. She was concerned for Mom,
and you too. Maybe if you had gone to Themis for help,
Mom wouldn't have gone to that cockamamie—"

"Cockatrice."

"Whatever." I flap my hand, waving Mavis' correction
away. She grabs hold of my hand, holding it high. Forcing
me to look at her. I expect to see fury, but instead I see my
tough older sister...struggling not to cry.

"I know I screwed up with Mom. I should've been
watching her closer. I should've gotten her help..." She
releases me and turns away. After a long silence, she adds in
a quiet voice, "Edie, if you don't trust me anymore, I can't
blame you. But please at least think about all I've told you."

"Mavis..."

She turns around, head up, seemingly back to normal.
"I'll help you charter a boat."

"You don't have to," I tell her. "I flew here and can go
back the same way."

"Edie, no!" She looks thoroughly scandalized.

"It was totally dark out."

Mavis shakes her head. "Everyone has phones with
lights on them. And cameras. All it takes is for one person to
see you—" I am shocked when she throws her arms around
me. "Edie, I can't lose you too."

For a moment, the pain and anger and uncertainty all
disappear. My heart rises into my throat, making words
impossible. We stand there a long time, squeezing each
other in a tight hug. When we finally pull apart, I say the
one thing I know is true. "Mavis, I'm glad my favorite sister
is still alive."

"You being alive is the best news I've had in a year," she responds.

We grin at each other.

She walks me to the harbor and negotiates with a crew to take me back to the docks at the mainland. Instead of reminding her I do stuff like this for myself all the time, I relax. Once I do, it's actually nice to have someone else taking care of things. Being in charge, leading missions, having to make big life decisions...super sucks after a while. It's nice to get a break from it.

But when, I wonder, *will Mavis get a break?*

"Be safe! And careful going through the portals. The monsters have set traps at a lot of them."

"Oh, I'm aware." Wait. "Mavis, were the monsters working on a bio-weapon?" I ask. "Something that would make shifters unable to shift?"

Mavis shakes her head. "Shifters not able to shift? That sounds horrible. I don't think my people would do that, but maybe the splinter group did. I can ask around. Will you come back and see me? In a week?"

I give her a tight nod, still unsure how I feel about her. But then I give her a big hug. My emotions are all over the place. I wave to her as I sail away. Then some tourist edges his way in front of me to take a picture. I blow some hot air at the back of his neck and then try not to laugh as he quickly scurries away. Back in my spot, I am disappointed to see that Mavis is gone.

Until I spot a cat running along the sand.

———

W hen I return to the Academy, Cassie is waiting for me at the portal. I am so glad to see her, I almost start crying again.

"I saw you'd be here, and I knew you'd be crying," she tells me, handing me a wet-wipe. "But my vision wasn't showing me much else, so..."

It's not like Cassie to run out of words...at least the Cassie I used to know.

"So, I went to your room." She takes a big breath of air. "I know that Tina is sick, and I know what that means. She was so pissed at me for showing up, she told Vee to bite me."

"Sounds like her spirits have improved a little," I say.

"Yes, well..." Cassie goes quiet again, and I nudge her.

"Out with it."

"I had to dodge Vee—I had no idea her neck could extend that far—and I accidentally knocked some stuff off your dresser. A mug broke, so I stuck it in the drawer, and..."

Tears form in Cassie's eyes. I put a hand on her shoulder.

"Don't worry, that mug had no sentimental value."

"It's not that! It's...I saw your picture, with your family!" Cassie says suddenly, the words pouring out now. "I saw... Emmie. I had no idea when you talked about your sister Mavis that she was Emmie."

"Yeah," I mutter. "Me neither. It's been a long week."

She offers me a small smile. She's changed so much from the chatterbox I used to know.

"Cassie, you can always talk to me," I tell her. "About anything. Even about what the monsters did to you."

She only shrugs and pulls out from under my touch. It hurts, but I know I need to give her time.

"What did I miss while I was gone?" I ask.

"Priapus' many descriptions of breasts—sorry, he calls

them ta-tas. A bunch of grapes was my personal favorite. But he worked his way up to melons."

"No..." I can just imagine Larissa meticulously drawing various fruit-shaped breasts.

"Don't worry, I covered for you. Said you had female problems. Actually, he seemed really confused by that until I said you were having issues with your hoo-hoo." She hands me a vial. "I also had Fern whip up one of her super energy potions; you're gonna need it to get through Maddox's class."

"You know I love you, right?" I gulp it down, managing not to wince at the bitter taste. Almost immediately I feel better. All my exhaustion is gone, and my wings pop out a bright shade of manic yellow.

"We'd better go." She starts to walk and motions for me to follow.

"Wait, I gotta check on Tina."

"Val's with her right now. He's wearing a T-shirt that says *Kiss My Grits*, which makes me think he's not worried about cutting. But Val is a rebel and you are not. And we both know Maddox won't take 'female troubles' as an excuse to miss her class."

That's the truth. Maddox will probably just tell me it boosts my rage, or something.

By the time we make it to the amphitheater, it is filled to bursting. Maddox is in the middle of another rousing speech. Someone yells at me to put my wings away because I'm blocking the stage. Not that there's anything new to see. Just Maddox, beating on her pulpit—er, podium—again.

There's a map behind her, projected on the wall, with a skull and crossbones marking something. As she talks, Maddox uses a big old ruler to point at it. "This particular group of monsters is responsible for the assault on this very academy."

Wait, is that the splinter group Mavis was talking about? I thought Nico wiped them out when we rescued Cassie? There must be more than one cell at work.

"Remember the students we lost that night?" Maddox asks, her voice suddenly dropping low. "Remember Felix?"

The map behind Maddox disappears, replaced by the smiling face of a werewolf boy who I saw torn in half that night.

"Remember Alyana?" Maddox asks, and the picture changes again, this time showing the cat-shifter I managed to save from being crushed to death by a cyclops, but whose spine was damaged. They sent her home in a wheelchair. The Academy put her out to the curb like trash. They have no use for a shifter who can't fight.

"Remember Darcy?" Maddox asks, and there behind her, smiling, happy, and very much alive, is the merman Cassie loved.

I glance at her, but her eyes are cast downward.

Maddox pounds on the podium. "We will attack. We will fight. We will destroy. Let them show pictures of *their* dead. It's their turn to *mourn!*"

The applause is deafening. I feel sickened by everyone's glee at the thought of a battle. But also strangely pumped. My wings explode from my back, a dark, deep red. No one yells at me to put them away this time. In fact, someone yells, "Yeah, we got a dragon on our side!"

I tuck my wings back away, ashamed. The dragon in me instinctually wants things that the human part of me is sickened by.

After the excitement dies down, Maddox tells everyone that they will get their marching orders from Nico after class. She then goes on to demonstrate, on Kratos, the best ways to incapacitate without killing.

"Hamstring," she shouts as she goes low and knocks Kratos on his ass. "Now, if I flip him on his stomach and sever his spine, he cannot move and I can question him at my leisure."

Kratos glares up at her when she mimics severing his spine, but even he is too intimidated to do more than that.

"Edie," someone says behind me and I whirl to find Nico. All the things that Mavis told me fly through my mind. That he loved her. That she nearly killed him. It's so messed up.

"You're on my team, dragon." He offers me a toothy grin.

"What?"

"For the raid," he explains. "I made sure you were on the strike team. I'm the leader."

"Raid? Like *kill*?"

I'm stunned. Students aren't allowed to go on combat missions. I had to downplay all the killing done during our unauthorized mission to get Cassie, afraid that we'd get in trouble.

Nico's grin disappears. Clearly, he'd expected high fives instead of questions. "Mr. Zee can see now that our students are soft. The way those monsters got the jump on all of you at the Spring Fling was embarrassing."

"You weren't even there, Nico!"

His eyes go wide with pretend innocence. "I'm just repeating what Mr. Zee said."

I roll my eyes. "Mr. Zee...or your mom."

"Maybe it was her suggestion," Nico shrugs several times. Almost like a twitch. I've flustered him. "And she'll be there, of course. Advising. But *I'll* be the leader." Before I can even mention the gross nepotism at work, he quickly adds,

"Mr. Zee chose me because I set a tracker on one of the monsters. That's how we know where to find them. And, well, I also know how to kill monsters."

Beside me, Cassie has gone even more pale, and stone still. "Are you going to kill them all?" she asks between clenched teeth.

"I hope I get the chance," Nico says, puffing out his chest.

Cassie whirls on him. "If I'd known...if I'd only seen how it would end up. Oh, Nico. I had a vision of you with a baby monster and I thought you'd changed." She rubs her eyes with clenched fists as if she's seeing it again, and it hurts.

"Cassie, I'm—" He reaches a hand to her, and it sounds like an apology is ready to come out. But Cassie shrinks away while at the same time Maddox booms from behind, "No mercy!"

Nico's whole body changes as he looks toward his mother. And a little of the light goes out of his remaining eye. "MOA is a school of war. You were raised here, Cassie. You should understand that. And you should also know there's only one way any of this ends." Cassie's eyes well up with tears, and Nico pauses for a moment, before pushing on. "Have a vision of *this*. Me, standing on a mountain of monster corpses. That's always been the endgame."

"Tone it down a notch," I tell him as Cassie starts to shake. "Look, I'm going to take her to the infirmary. We'll talk about the raid later, okay?"

"Wait, I'll help you." He puts a hand on Cassie's arm, looking genuinely concerned.

"Nooooo!" A shrill, frightened scream comes out of Cassie. I quickly step between her and Nico—popping my wings out to create a wall between us.

Putting an arm around Cassie, I half carry her to medical.

I breathe a sigh of relief when I spot Fern speaking with Greg and Jordan in their corner of the sick room. I wave to get her attention and she hurries to us.

"What's wrong?" she asks, immediately looking Cassie over.

"I don't know."

Cassie's eyes are vacant and her skin is clammy. "I think the monsters..." No. That's not right. I need to say what I really think. "I think when we rescued her she was traumatized. We...oh gods...we killed so many."

Fern bites her lower lip to stop it from trembling. "And I helped you," she says sadly, as she gently reaches toward Cassie who immediately leans on her. "I'll see what can be done."

"Wait!" I catch her eye again. "Tina?" I ask quietly.

"She's not bad. Not good either. We'll talk later."

I watch as she leads Cassie away, feeling like the worst friend ever. I should've done more. I should've...

I don't know what I should've done.

I join Greg and Jordan.

"Is Cassie okay?" Greg asks.

"I don't know," I tell him, sitting at the foot of his bed. "If anyone can help her, Fern will. How are you guys?"

Jordan hasn't even looked up. He's busy scribbling in a notebook.

"Fine," Greg grumbles. "Except..."

"Hey, Edie, what rhymes with -itis?" Jordan asks, his head bowed over whatever he is writing.

"Um...lots of diseases, I guess?"

"Yeah, no. Those won't work."

"What's happening?" I ask Greg.

"Jordan's writing a love poem to Hepa," Greg informs me. "He wants her back. And he wants her to tickle his belly again."

"When I'm a panther," Jordan inserts. Then he grins in a goofy love-struck sort of way. "She found the tickle-spot that makes my back leg go all thumpery."

"Wait, didn't she break up with him a while ago?"

"Yeah, but then Jordan got sick and convinced Hepa to give him a second chance. But then, many makeups and breakups later—all of which, mind you, happened in this very room—Hepa called it quits for good. You've missed a lot, Edie," Greg tells me. "It's like a soap opera in here."

I laugh. "Really? I could use some drama that's not mine."

"Well," he lowers his voice to sound like a TV announcer. "When last we saw our lovebirds, Hepa was angry that Jordan would not give up everything to be with her."

"Right, I was here for that episode featuring the inter-species dating ban," I say with a stilted laugh.

"Then in a shocking twist," he continues, "Jordan decides that he is a one-woman man."

"I don't believe you." My laugh is louder now. Gods, I missed my friends.

"It's true," Jordan chimes in. "Hepa is the only girl for me."

"The problem is," Greg explains, "Hepa says she's over him."

"The thrill was in the chase?"

"But I'm gonna win her back," Jordan says. "With poetry."

I shake my head. "Should I even ask?"

"Please don't," Greg begs.

"Don't be a hater," Jordan tells him, then mumbles, "tis, biz, jizz." He glances down at his paper then scribbles something else. "Okay guys, I got it."

"Let's hear." I steel myself. Please don't let this be a poem about jizz.

He clears his throat. "Roses are red. Violets are blue. Hepatitis, I love you."

Greg and I eye each other, then burst out laughing.

"What?" Jordan asks.

"No, it's great," I tell him. "I'm sure Hepa will love it."

"Look, you try coming up with a rhyme for her name..." He looks so crestfallen. "It's really hard."

"Kiss!" Greg shouts suddenly. "Rhyme Hepatitis with 'wants to kiss'!"

"Oh," Jordan grins. "That's good."

Greg rolls his eyes. "This is what we've been doing. It's so booooring, Edie. What's going on in the outside world?"

"Nothing good."

I fill him in on the raid Maddox has planned and the students' fanatical reactions. "Basically, Maddox is the cult leader and too many around here have drunk the Kool-Aid."

"Um...Edie..." Greg says, but I'm on a roll and don't let him interrupt.

"It's pretty gross."

"Nico..." Greg says.

"Yes, Nico! He's just as bad. I mean, he's super-hot. He's even got that tortured moody boy thing going for him. But I can't even get into how complicated it is right now."

Jordan looks up, past my shoulder. "Oh, hey Nico."

I close my eyes. "He's behind me, isn't he?"

"I tried to tell you," Greg says.

I turn and find Nico smirking. He definitely heard the

part about me calling him super-hot. Hopefully he didn't hear me talking smack about his mom.

"My mother..." he starts. Shit, maybe he did hear that. "...wants to meet you."

"Huh?" I say dimly.

"I told my mom about you. Our mission to get Cassie. And about you being a dragon. She wants to meet you."

"Now?" I ask, panicked.

"No, at dinner. We're invited to the faculty dining hall."

"No fair!" Jordan says. "They have the best food. I've been eating hospital grub for a week."

"Take my place," I mutter.

Nico shakes his head. "This invitation is non-transfer-able." He leans in. "And my mother doesn't like to be stood up."

"Not so much an invitation as a mandate, then?" I say.

"Don't worry." Nico graces me with a wicked grin. "I'll be there to protect you from the 'cult leader.'"

Greg lets out a little terrified squeak on my behalf.

Crap. I really put my foot in my mouth.

"I was just venting," I explain. "I'm sure your mom is great, once I meet her in person."

Nico doesn't seem angry, though, just amused.

"It's actually a nice change from everyone being afraid of her. And Mom already told me she likes your spunk. But don't be late," he warns me. "She noticed you were tardy to class, and was not pleased."

I give him a salute and he saunters away.

"That guy definitely has mommy issues," Greg says.

"Yeah, for sure," Jordan agrees. "I mean, can you imagine having Mad Maddox for a mom?"

"Nico isn't that bad..." Greg and Jordan give me a look.

"Guys, he was tortured for, like, a year. Give him some credit!"

"Just be careful at dinner," Greg says. "Once that guy's got a scent, he won't let it go."

I gulp, thinking of how he followed Mavis all the way to Greece. When she spoke about him she was genuinely scared. I don't want to be on his radar, much less his fanatical mother's.

Too late for that. I just hope they don't serve Kool-Aid at dinner.

27

Before dinner, I check on Tina.

Unlike the shifters, who had an initial few days of sickness then recovered without the ability to shift, Tina isn't recovering. The transfusions of vampire blood she's getting are the only thing that help to perk her up, but it's getting harder and harder for us to cover her absences.

"Where were you?" Val asks as soon as I walk into the room.

"I just stopped by the infirmary to check on Jordan and Greg and—"

"No." Val coldly interrupts. "Where were you when you disappeared for almost two whole days?"

I blink. Taken aback by his tone and that he noticed I was missing. I glance at Tina, who's buried beneath a layer of blankets. "Maybe we should go outside and talk about this."

He nods his assent and we quietly exit the room together. We remain silent as Val takes the lead down the hallway. When we reach the front entrance instead of heading out the door, Val grabs my hand, tugging me in the other direction.

The dormitory buildings are assigned according to students' disciplines. Assassination class in one building, healers in another, and so on. Each building is then split in half, with the boys on one side and girls on the other. And Val right now is taking me into the boys' assassination dorm. Which means he's taking me to his bedroom.

I hesitate. "Um, I don't really know if I should—"

Val's lips twitch with amusement. "Edie, I'm not taking you to my room to put the moves on you." He pauses and lifts his eyebrows. "Unless you want me to."

"No! I..." I stop because I do sorta want Val to put the moves on me. It would be a nice distraction from all the stuff with Mavis swirling around in my head. And Nico's upcoming raid isn't making me feel so great either. At the same time, things with Val are complicated too.

"Look," Val says, cutting through my confusion. "We need to talk privately. If we go outside there's a good chance Nico will run into us again. Or run into me, should I say. It's obvious the guy is tracking you."

"He is not," I protest. "You make him sound like a stalker."

"No, he's much worse. He's a wolf with your scent. I saw him sniffing around the portal after you went missing yesterday." Val tugs my hand again, and this time I follow him down the hall to his room. He opens the door and holds it open for me.

Still nervous, I go back to the Nico argument. "You know, he's planning this big raid. That's probably why he was at the portal."

Val shakes his head. "No. He was hunting."

"Okay, well—" I push past Val into his room and all words leave me. His room is so him.

Three of the walls are painted black. But the fourth is a mural that's a bright mix of colors. I walk over, wanting to examine it more closely. I see Val riding a unicorn through a night sky filled with pizzas instead of stars. In another connecting scene he's cliff-diving from the top of a waterfall that goes from the ceiling all the way down to the floor. His bare white butt shimmers slightly.

"This is amazing," I laugh.

"Yeah. While I was being introduced to all of Larissa's family and friends, Tina snuck back to campus. I think she wanted to check on Vee—"

"Of course she did," I interject.

"But she also wanted to cheer me up. So"—Val indicates the entire wall—"she did this. Or most of it. Before she got sick, she was coming in almost every day to add more."

"Okay, just to clarify. We are talking about the same Tina, right? Your twin sister. Who only smiles when she's laughing at someone else's misfortune?"

Val shrugs. "She has hidden depths."

"Yeah, speaking of those..." Uncomfortable, I sit down. Then realizing I'm sitting on Val's bed, I spring up again.

I don't know how eyes as dark as Val's can laugh. But his do.

And right now—they're laughing at me.

Sticking my chin up, I sit back down on his bed. And then primly cross my ankles and fold my hands in my lap. Val actually bursts out laughing at this, which feels like winning a prize. I grin back at him before remembering what I was about to say.

"Tina told me about her mixed blood. And plant powers. Oh, and I heard all about your family too. She was really out of it and just sort of talking...but I think maybe it also felt really good to get it off her chest."

Val nods tightly and then turns away from me to study his mural wall.

"I don't need to ask if you'll keep her secret," he says at last. "I know you will."

"Of course," I answer immediately.

He turns back to me, his face tight. "You know then that I'm a Moggy too."

"Yeah and I don't care about it, either. I think the whole Moggy thing is stupid."

"So do I. But Tina...she's always craved acceptance and is determined to be accepted into the crème de la crème of vampire society, even though she knows they're a bunch of inbred jerks."

Val sits beside me on the bed, his weight tipping me towards him. Our shoulders bump together. I'm not gonna act like an idiot again and jump away, so instead I just go with it, relaxing until his left side from shoulder to hip connects with my right side from shoulder to hip.

"Val," I say softly, looking straight ahead at the amazing mural while feeling Val's cold seep into me. "You have powers too, don't you?"

Even as I speak the air surrounding us becomes thick with fog. At first it's so light, I blink, wondering if I'm imagining it. But then the fog grows and Val's whole room is swallowed in white. If he wasn't pressed against me, I'd have no idea if he was even in the room anymore.

I remember then how it rained the day we talked last semester when I was feeling homesick for Florida. It was a tiny cloud, like it had been made just for me. And then again in the desert, when Val found me, it rained. That was Val.

"Yes, Edie," Val answers at last. "I have powers."

I kiss him then and Val wastes no time kissing me back. His arms come around me, pulling me tight against him so more of me is connected to more of him. As we sink back onto the bed, it feels like Val and I are in our own space, and all the rules are suspended.

Val trails kisses along my lips and then gently bites the soft skin at the corner of my mouth. I shriek in surprise.

"Sorry," he says, pulling away. "It's a vampire thing."

Grabbing hold of his T-shirt I jerk him toward me. "I liked it. Do it again."

His eyes grow dark as he descends once more. I squeal again because it's weird and wonderful that I'm kissing a vampire and it's Val and—

Bam.

The person next door bangs on the adjoining wall.

"Val. Can you and Larissa give it a break already?"

I go still. The cold is no longer coming from Val, but growing outward from my own center. The room is no longer our foggy world away from the world. It's just a dorm room again...one where everything, including me, is slightly damp.

Bringing my knees up, I push Val away.

"Edie." He's on his feet instantly, extending a hand to where I'm still pushing myself up off his bed.

Ignoring his hand, I stand. "No. I cannot believe I let you play me like this."

He crosses his arms. "My next door neighbor is an idiot. Yes, Larissa has been in my room. We talk. Sometimes we play chess. It's a shared passion."

"Shared passion? Interesting word choice, Val." I shove my way past him, to march out the door, but Val snags the back of my shirt. "Let me go. I may not be able to burn you, but I can make this room awful toasty for you."

"Edie, I can't let you go."

Val reels me in using my shirt as the fishing twine, until my back is attached to his front. Wrapping both his arms around me, his cool breath hits my neck. "I told myself that when I returned to campus with Larissa, I wouldn't see you. Wouldn't talk to you. But then you were lost in the desert and I kept going through portal after portal trying to find you. I had to. The thought of never seeing you again..." He sighs and a shiver runs down my spine. "Edie, I can't let you go."

"Oh." It takes a while after that before I'm capable of words again. After that speech I feel like we should be running off hand in hand to our happily ever after. But my head isn't in the clouds anymore and I can see the future all too clearly. "You're still marrying Larissa."

"Yes," he answers without hesitation. "With Tina huddled away in her room for so long, already there's been talk. Whispers that she's sick with the shifter disease. Both Larissa and I are doing our best to crush them, but the longer she's gone..." Val sighs. "Her position is more precarious than ever—"

"And yours too," I can't help but point out.

I feel Val's head shake, his lips brush the back of my head. "If it was only me, I'd leave today. Derrick—my old roommate—and I used to talk about working private security. His uncle had a business, very exclusive. Monsters of all types worked for him. We figured we had the perfect education for it, since MOA is the perfect place for learning how to protect rich and lazy idiots."

I can't help but think of how the gods hid behind tables during the Spring Fling massacre, and agree with Val.

I allow myself one more minute within the protection of Val's arms before pulling away. "I have to go. I'm expected at this faculty dinner thing."

Val lets out a laugh.

"What?" I ask.

"Kratos invited me to attend as well." He holds open the door for me. "Shall we?"

I follow hesitantly. There's no getting away from Val.

28

Val leads the way to the faculty dining hall. During class he tends to sit at the back of the classroom. When I glance back at him (one or twenty times per class) he usually looks either amused or disinterested. But all the teachers love him anyway. Other than his attitude, he's the perfect student, easily acing every assignment.

Val holds one of the heavy double doors for me. Inside I see nothing but gloom. But that instantly transforms when I pass through the doorway. Suddenly, it's like I'm still outside —but in a beautiful Grecian garden.

White pillars with creeping vines stand in a circle around stone tables set with grapes, wine, and food. On a dais is a taller table with the more "important" teachers and Zee's guests of honor. It looks like a wedding party, or the Last Supper, with Zee in the middle gazing down on everything.

To his left is Themis, and to her side, Kratos. On his right are Maddox and Priapus. I guess the students are meant to sit across from the teacher who chose them because Nico sits across from Zee and waves me over to take the seat across from his mother.

Val goes to his place across from Kratos without another word. I cross through the "lesser tables" and nod at some teachers I recognize from around campus but haven't had any classes with yet. There's an empty chair that has Hermes' name gilded onto it, but he's not here yet. Finally, I squeeze in between Nico and Larissa. She grins at me.

"I didn't know you would also be here," she says.

"Maddox invited me," I hazard a glance at her. She's studying me so intently it makes me shiver. I reach for my wine glass, hoping it's filled with something that will take the edge off.

"And Priapus invited you?" I ask.

I sip the wine and it's so smooth and fruity, it has to be magical—possibly ambrosia. I've heard that the gods' self-healing powers are derived from that drink, and that a few years ago a shifter—jealous of the vamp's ability to never age—got it in his head to swipe some from the gods' table. Apparently, all it did was give him a stomachache and a painful erection for a solid week.

"Oh yes, Priapus invited me. He says that I am his best student," she tells me excitedly. "He was very impressed with my dedication to anatomy—and with my drawings of... how do you say? The hoo-hoo!"

I spit my wine into my napkin and cough.

"Are you okay?" Zee asks me.

"Yes, of course."

"That liquid is the nectar of the gods," Zee tells me. "Ambrosia. Watered down for human consumption."

"I thought that was a kind of sweet salad," Larissa says. "With marshmallows. No?"

"It is," I tell her kindly, "just not in this context."

"Sorry I'm late," Hepa runs up to the table, taking her seat at the end, across from Themis and next to Val. "Metis has all the healers working overtime on a cure for the shifters."

"Any progress?" Val asks.

Hepa gives a tight shake of her head.

"I'm sure that Metis will figure it out," Themis says. "It's only a matter of time."

"Yeah, that stubborn bitch won't stop until she has a cure," Zee agrees.

Nico leans in and whispers to me, "Zee and Metis used to be married."

"That was a *very* long time ago," Zee tells me with a wink. "The things one gets up to in their youth. Did you know I once had an orgy with Cerberus and a centaur? Those were the days!"

"Indeed!" Priapus agrees with a raise of his glass. "That's when you could wang noodle a hippogriff and no one would say boo!"

"Edie," Zee's focus is back on me. "I wonder if maybe you and I should do some private tutoring? We need to understand what you can do in your dragon form."

I don't like the lecherous way that he's looking at me. Themis must not either, because she appears at Zee's shoulder.

She lifts his empty glass from the table. "Zee, let me get you more ambrosia. You seem thirsty tonight."

"Oh, yes. We *are* celebrating after all."

"There is nothing to celebrate yet," Maddox speaks for the first time and all eyes are on her.

Over her shoulder, though, I notice Themis slipping something into Zee's glass. It's so quick, I wonder if I'm imagining it. The thing is, my sight is stellar. Above 20/20.

Grandma's optometrist used to jokingly refer to me as, "A freak." I guess it's another dragon thing. When Themis sees me looking her way, our eyes meet. She gives a tight shake of the head and then holds a finger to her lips. It's the classic symbol for, 'let's keep this secret between us.'

So that's weird.

But also just another day at Mount Olympus.

"My son told me a lot about you," Maddox says, drawing my attention to the table once more, where suddenly, all eyes are on me. "You saved his life."

"That was more of an accident..." I mumble.

Is it hot in here, or is it just the intensity of Maddox's gaze?

"Don't be humble. It's a fear emotion. And fear is weakness."

I know my role here is simply to smile and nod at everything Maddox says. No matter how crazy it might be. But honestly? I'm not in the mood today.

"My mom used to say, 'There are no wrong emotions. Own them all or they'll own you.'" My throat thickens. At the end Mom obviously forgot this bit of advice, because she let grief get the best of her.

"How stupid," Maddox says dismissively. "I hope your time at Mount Olympus has begun to offset such awful advice."

I set my glass down with more force than necessary. "Actually—"

Nico cuts me off before I can say anymore. "Edie's an amazing warrior. You should've seen her when we rescued Cassie—"

"That was an unsanctioned mission," Themis says.

"Better to ask for forgiveness than for permission." Nico gives Themis one of his best grins.

Maddox smiles at this. "And that is what Nico's mother taught him."

I roll my eyes. She acts like she made that saying up.

Maddox is too busy taking a swig of ambrosia to notice. After wiping her mouth with the back of her hand, she gives a sharp clap. "I'm ravenous. Let's eat."

"Yes, of course," Zee motions for the servants—various sprites—to serve us. The largest platter has an actual whole boar with an apple in its mouth. It smells delicious, and the meat falls apart on my plate. My mouth waters.

"Artemis and I brought down this family of boars ourselves," Maddox says. "They screamed for mercy as my teeth ripped out their throats one by one."

Holy Hades. I've never understood vegetarians more than I do right now.

Larissa must feel the same way—she picks at the grapes on her plate. Nico, on the other hand, digs right in, apparently committing some table manner *faux paus* because I hear Val mutter, "*dog.*"

Nico spits a bone onto his plate and looks up at his mom. "Tell us the story of that vampire you killed, the one that got you kicked out of the Academy."

"That's not exactly dinner table conversation," Maddox says, but with a grin that lets us know she'd be happy to tell us.

"Actually, Maddox, why don't you tell us about what you've been up to since that rather memorable event?" Themis easily slides into the conversation. "I hadn't heard much about you until Zee invited you to guest lecture this summer."

"Oh, a bit of this and a bit of that," she says, but a little of the satisfaction that usually oozes from every word has disappeared.

Nico bumps Val's elbow, just as he's about to take a drink. Ambrosia splatters down the front of his shirt. It's one of my favorites of his. There's a picture of a giant cactus and next to it the words: *Don't Be A Prick*.

"My bad," Nico says with a giant smile.

"Don't worry about it," Val says, his voice pitched low and dangerous. "It's tight quarters. These things happen." Calmly picking up a napkin, he dabs at his shirt.

My shoulders relax as it seems like maybe there won't be a brawl.

But then Val's hand becomes a blur as he sets his napkin back down and the next thing I know the apple that had been in the boar's mouth is now filling Nico's.

Nico's jaws clench, smashing the apple and sending juice rushing down his chin.

Larissa giggles. A soft titter, barely audible over Nico's growl. But his head immediately whips in her direction.

"I am sorry," she says, both hands over her mouth. "It is just Val's cleverness." One of her small hands covers Val's. "He made *you* the boar after you *were* a boor. Yes?" She looks at Val, eyes wide and uncertain. "You were meaning to be funny, Val? Joshing, as they say?"

Nico's growl gets louder and it's obvious from the bursting of the neckline of his shirt that he's on the verge of changing.

"Don't shift where you eat," Kratos says, standing and planting both of his giant hands on the table. His gaze shifts from Nico to run down the entire length of our side of the table. "Kids, play nice." So we understand it's not advice, but an order, he flexes his biceps a few times before sitting down again.

"I'm surprised you allow vampire trash at the dinner table," Maddox says to Mr. Zee, her eyes still locked on Val's.

He gives her the Val special, sleepy eyes with a half-smile. Like he doesn't even care. But I can see how tense his whole body is, and I wonder what it costs him to have so much control. Maddox shifts her attention to Larissa, who immediately shrinks away. "And how did this girl even get into Mount Olympus? She can barely speak English."

A little gasp comes out of Larissa and Val reaches over to comfort her. I quickly look away.

"Everyone, everyone," Themis says, coming to Maddox's elbow. "Let's try to remember that we're all on the same side."

"Party Pooper," Maddox says in a low voice, obviously meant for Mr. Zee's ears.

He giggles and then hiccups.

Themis' hand lands on his shoulder. "Right, Zee?"

"Huh?" Mr. Zee asks. "Yes, of course," he agrees, finally.

Larissa looks at me, her light eyes full of hurt. "Trash? This is not an American word for vampire, is it?"

A sudden rush of hot anger fills my stomach. "They're not trash," I say, just as Maddox is taking her seat. "They're here to learn, and to fight, just like the rest of us."

Maddox's gaze melts my anger. I'd thought that I was locking horns with her earlier, but she was just playing with me. This, though, is the real thing. Fear, a cold, hard dead thing, fills my gut and makes me believe I'll never be able to make fire again.

"The vampires have long been selfish creatures," she tells me. "They are for themselves. Either you are with us, or you are our enemy. And death comes to my enemies."

"Whoa, things are intense up here," Hermes says, appearing behind Zee and breaking the tension. "Death and enemies all before dessert?"

"Yes," Priapus says, nodding towards me. "This hoo-hoo

holder is right. Vampires and shifters are only exterior clas-sifications. It's inside that counts. And what's underneath!" He motions to his ginormous penis—and gods help me, my eyes automatically follow the movement. That's when I discover his dick currently rests on the back of a Shetland pony under the table.

Mr. Zee laughs, and smacks Priapus on the back. "Speaking of which, that thing you wanted arranging...I took care of it."

"What is this?" Themis asks.

"Oh, just a little trip for the boys," Zee says with grin. "A field trip."

"No field trip was approved." Themis sounds panicked now.

"Not for the students," Hermes assures her. "Teachers only."

"Yes, we're going to..." Zee looks befuddled. "Where are we going to again?" he asks. I think of what Themis snuck into his wine. Does that have something to do with his memory loss?

"We're going to a strip club!" Hermes announces loudly.

"Oh yes, that's right." Zee nods, taking another drink from his glass.

"I heard the Florida ones were especially *nasty*," Priapus tells us gleefully.

"Well, have fun with that," I mutter.

"It's for the best that it's not for students anyway," Nico says, with a yawn. "I have too much prep to do. My team has a raid in two days."

"Wait, we *do*?" I ask, but Hermes cuts me off.

"Children," he says, shaking his head. "They don't know how to properly party."

Kratos raises his glass. "Drink and be merry, for tomorrow we may die!"

There's a round of 'here, heres' that sound perfunctory to my ears. Of course, most of the faculty are gods—and they will never die.

"Oh, I have a splendid idea," Zee says, slurring slightly. "You," he points to Val, "and you," he motions to Larissa, "Should be on Nico's strike team. Bring the species together!"

"Yes, that's exactly right!" Priapus jumps in. "Bring the students together. Let them learn intimacy on the battlefield, instead of the bedroom. That's how we stop them from crossbreeding with all their boom-boom, dinky-tickling, hibbity-dibbity, doodle-bopping, fenorking, humpy squirty, knobbing, jiggery pokery, organ grinding, porking, quelching, rip-n-dip, or—well, there are students present and I don't want to confuse them, so let me finish with the proper terminology—schnoodlypooping."

Mr. Zee looks drunk. And confused. "What in the gods are you going on about?"

"Sex!" Hermes bursts out. "His wealth of knowledge is a gift to us all."

"Yes, of course. I knew that! I wanted to ensure everyone else was following. It must be clear to all that Moggies are no longer accepted at Mount Olympus Academy." Zee is definitely drunk. And Priapus is not far behind. "Good thing we're having the vamps test for Moggies along with the shifter plague. I'm thinking of making them wear armbands next semester or some such thing."

"You're what?" I ask.

My blood was tested. If it turns out I'm a Moggy, I could've been outed to everyone. But Val tested me and he wouldn't say anything, even if he knew. I glance up, but he avoids my gaze. What about the rest of the shifters who are mixed? Are they in danger?

"I'm not comfortable adding vampires to my team," Nico starts but Maddox cuts him off.

"You should be comfortable commanding vampires. They are lesser beings."

"This is too much," Themis says, tossing down her fork. "If we can't even have a nice dinner—" She's interrupted when Metis rushes into the dining hall.

"I've done it!" she announces. "I found a cure for the plague!"

29

Even watered down the ambrosia leaves me feeling a little hungover the next morning. Or maybe it was all the rich food. Or it could've been the amount of tension around that table. Put that in a bottle and you could power all of Florida for a year.

Shading my eyes against the too bright sun, I make my way across campus to the infirmary. The healers strictly sealed off the building while they were dosing the afflicted shifters with the cure—a serum that Metis concocted using antibodies from the dead baby scorpion. When I arrive, they've just begun to allow non-afflicted students in.

Rochelle—the lion-shifter who had been stuck in her cat form—is in a circle of friends, restored to her human body. She doesn't seem able to speak, though. Every time she opens her mouth, all that comes out is a guttural rumble.

"It'll pass," Hepa says, appearing at my side. "But it will take time for her higher functions to return."

"Greg? And Jordan?" I ask, nervously.

"Jordan never had any higher functions," Hepa

responds. "So he's fine. As is your little bat-man. I sent them both back to their dorms last night after dosing them."

"Thank gods," I say, relief flooding me.

"Edie!" Fern calls for me from across the room and I make my way to her, slipping past beds with former patients who are shifting in and out of their forms, ecstatic to be able to change again.

"We did it!" Fern says, a huge smile on her face. "Or, well, Metis did. But it couldn't have happened without you. Metis wouldn't let anyone near the little scorpion monster you found. She was the only one allowed to work with it, and she said its venom is still incredibly dangerous, even now."

She takes my arm, leading me back through the crowd of departing, healthy shifters. "Metis asked Merilee to lock up the scorpion body deep in the Archives, for further study at some point. The shifter plague wasn't any normal illness; the monsters made it as a bio-weapon. Metis is curious if she can reverse engineer it now."

I stop in my tracks, disturbed. "What does that mean?"

"Well," Fern says. "If the monsters can make a plague that makes shifters unable to shift, maybe we can create our own. One that would turn a regular human into a shifter. We wouldn't have to count on students being born as shifters then. We could just make them."

"Um, that's kind of horrible," I tell her. "And I say that as someone who totally thought she was just a regular human until she found out she was a shifter. It's sort of traumatic."

"Oh, yeah. Totally!" Fern says. "I'm sorry...I wasn't thinking about it that way. I was just excited about the science of it."

"It's okay," I tell her, but I don't have time to argue

medical ethics. "Listen... do you think you can get me some of the—"

"Already ahead of you," Fern says, slipping a vial into my hand. "For Tina, right? One dose should do it. But because we don't know what percentage of her heritage is shifter, it could be...messy."

"Messy, how?" I do share living space with her, after all.

"Messy like...well, just maybe don't use the same bathroom for a few days."

"Great, thanks," I mutter, tucking the vial into my backpack. "Gotta run. Kratos hates it when people are late."

He definitely does. He also hates it more now that Maddox is considered the official on-campus badass. He's spent the last few classes just showing us how much he can deadlift.

But today looks different. As I slide into my seat right before the start of class, I see that his weights are no longer at the front of the classroom. Instead, there's a god I don't know standing next to Kratos.

"I understand some of you are going on a mission tomorrow?" Kratos asks. Nico nods, as do a few other heads —my fellow teammates, Larissa and Val among them.

"Wonderful," Kratos says. "I thought now would be a good time to review stabbing techniques, and I've brought Algos, the god of pain, here to illustrate a few things."

Algos gives us all a steely nod. He's beautiful in a weepy, tortured poet kind of way. Skinny, but with the toned body of a runner. He's got his blond hair tied back in a man-bun and he looks like he's about to whip out a guitar and sing about his lost love. Total hipster hottie.

Except he doesn't even get a chance to introduce himself before Kratos stabs him in the gut.

We all gasp.

Algos holds onto Kratos for support as he doubles over, blood dripping off the end of the dagger still sticking out of Algos' body.

"Now," Kratos says, "a gut wound is almost always fatal, but it takes time, and your enemy will still have opportunities to harm others on the field. Unless you totally gut them."

With that, Kratos sweeps the dagger out of Algos' midsection, tracing a half circle from which all of his intestines fall out. A cat-shifter vomits and runs out of the room, but Algos is already leaning over, gathering up his own guts in his arms.

Amazingly, a look of pure pleasure is on his face. "Again?" His tone is sweet like a child asking for another push on the swing.

"Perv," someone mutters.

"No, next we work on heart removal," Kratos says, and Algos nods excitedly as he pulls open the empty cavity of his abdomen and stuffs his intestines back inside. He holds both hands over his belly as a healer holds a glass of ambrosia to his lips. He takes two sips and within seconds, a warm glow envelops Algos. Just like that, he's back to normal.

And alarmingly sad again.

"Someone stab me," he pleads. "Please?"

It's like that for the rest of the hour, students taking turns finding out what it will feel like to run their blade up against bone, gouge out an eye, and partially decapitate someone.

Larissa and Cassie slip out together almost immediately.

Val handles the decapitation like a professional. Usually I like his coldness, but in this context—it's scary.

Nico is worse, though. His single eye glows as he stabs Algos repeatedly.

I'm up after him. To make this "fun," Kratos has set up two urns. We reach into the first one to pick a body part. The second urn tells us what weapon to use.

I reach in and hope for something not too icky. Feeling too sick to eat breakfast this morning was lucky, because otherwise I definitely would've thrown up by now. I pull out the paper and unfold it.

BALLS

Aw crap.

I hold it out so the rest of the class can see. Algos claps his hands in excitement as I reach into urn number two. My second paper is even worse than the first.

BARE HANDS

"Oh, this is going to be so much fun!" Algos squeals.

I shudder. "Can you please stop talking, Algos? You're making it so much worse."

He smiles, his eyes going soft and dreamy. "Yeah, I get that a lot."

Kratos steps between us. "Edie! Less yacking, more castrating. Now there are several ways to do this. My personal favorite I call, 'making vino.' It's impossible to screw up. You just grab 'em and squeeze, the same way you'd pulp a grape."

I gag, bringing only bile up.

"Spit or swallow it back down," Kratos advises me, and then he goes back to describing castration techniques. "Now if you want to get a little more artistic with it, I'd recommend—"

That's it. I can't listen to any more of this. I shift, and then basically curl up inside of myself, letting the dragon take over. It doesn't take long. There's a horrible squishing noise, Algos screams with delight in a high soprano, and then I'm Edie again, my hands covered in—

Val stands in front of me. Shirtless. He rubs my gross hands clean with the same shirt that had just been on his body. It's cold. But warm too.

Kratos stands behind him, shaking his head at me. "It's a shame such a weak human has a dragon inside her. But your instincts are good. Let your dragon do what needs to be done." He turns to the rest of the class. "Alright, I think that's enough for now. Is everyone who's going on the mission prepared to use these lessons?"

I nod, hoping I don't have to castrate anyone with my bare hands as part of my day tomorrow. Or pretty much ever again.

"Good," Kratos says, and then dismisses us. "Best of luck!"

"And don't forget," Algos calls, rearranging his pants. "Always twist the knife so the wound can't close! Ta-ta, kiddos!"

———

I'm walking back to the dorm when Nico catches up to me.

"Are you ready for tomorrow?" he asks, tilting his head at me. "Or should I ask if your dragon is ready?"

"Oh thanks, Nico. That's hilarious. I see you took to heart all that 'twisting the knife' advice."

"Hey, you got it done, that's the important thing." Nico nods. "And it was great prep. Almost as good as one of Mom's speeches. Although I'm sure she'll give one at the portal."

"Yep," I say. "I'm sure of that, too."

"Hey," Nico grabs my arm, and it's all I can do not to turn away from him. But he does have puppy dog eyes...

well. Eye. But just that one is enough to make me melt a little.

"Look, I know my mom can be a little much sometimes," he says.

"A little much?" I ask. "She called Larissa and Val trash. Larissa is basically the nicest person I've ever met."

Nico's face hardens. "She laughed at me. My mom insisted on walking me back to the dorms after dinner because she was worried what might happen to the sissy boy she'd raised. She's killed vampires for smaller insults. I should've made sure that was the last time Larissa laughed."

"Nico. You don't really think that, do you?"

He swallows. "The first time we met she gave me a flower. She thought I looked sad and might like one. When I told her I was a werewolf, she wasn't scared, just...interested. Like she found it fascinating. Then she asked me if I was 'very much fluffy' as a werewolf. And if so, might she someday pet me." Nico shakes his head, rueful. "You know no one's ever asked me about my fluffiness before."

"Yeah, Larissa is special. She looks at the whole world with wonder."

Nico laughs, but not unkindly. "She's gonna be worse than useless on the mission tomorrow, though. I'll try and assign her somewhere out of the way. Keep her safe. The last thing I need is for her to be bumping into my mom on the battlefield."

"Definitely," I agree. Then, since Nico seems in a softer mood, I can't help but ask, "Are you really excited for this mission tomorrow? You really want to do more killing?"

He doesn't say anything for a long time, and I think he's offended. But then, softly, he says, "Everyone has a reason for being the way they are, you know?"

I think about Tina, back in our dorm, squirming under

blankets as the Moggy blood in her veins denies the pure-blooded vampire mask she's always tried to wear.

"Yeah, I get that."

"So, all I'm saying is, my mom has a fun side, too." Nico grins. "She actually juggles."

"She what?" I ask, astonished.

"Juggles. This one time, on a raid, she chopped off three Gorgon heads and—"

"Never mind," I interrupt him, glad we finally reached my dorm room. "Well, 'til tomorrow then—"

Nico grabs my hand. "Edie, my mom didn't hate you last night. In fact, I think she liked that you tried to stand up to her. She didn't say that in as many words, but when she mentioned all the people at the table last night who deserved to have their throats ripped out—she didn't mention your name."

He looks happy about this. Like it is great news that I maybe sorta kinda passed the first test.

Now Nico takes my other hand, so both of mine are sandwiched between his. He starts to rub them as he says, "I think we should go see Mr. Zee. Together. And ask him for a special allowance to date. No mating, of course. Not yet. Despite hating crossbreeding, I think he'd see how your dragon abilities crossed with all the benefits of my killer gene pool would—"

"Whoa. Nico. Slow down." I jerk my hands away.

"Edie, it's okay. I'm not scared. I know most of the guys at this school are all, 'no way am I banging a fire breathing girl,' but that's the part of you I like best."

I frantically reach behind me for the door handle. "Nico, I just remembered I have a homework assignment for Priapus. I failed the last quiz, so I have to write ten times, "I will not call the hoo-hoo a haha-are-you-kiddingme. I will not call the pee-pee the eighth dwarf, right after Sleepy."

"What? He's crazy," Nico says. "Just tell him you didn't do it because you had a mission to prepare for. My mom will write you an excuse."

"No, thanks. I'd rather just do it and be done." I push the door open and slip inside. "Night!" Quickly, I slam it in his face. And then breathe a long sigh of relief.

When I bring air in again, I realize how rank it smells.

How did Nico not scent that? Hopefully he doesn't think that's my normal dorm room funk. Or maybe hopefully he does. The guy doesn't seem capable of understanding that I might be less into him than he's into me.

Tina is buried in her blankets. When I uncover her, she looks like a hot mess. Her hair is greasy and plastered to her forehead. Her skin is pale and clammy. And the room funk is definitely wafting off her.

She isn't exactly thrilled when I wake her up to offer the vial.

"It's the cure," I try to explain, but she only glares at me.

"Or it's an evil plot to take my fangs out," she snarls, snatching the vial from me.

"Tina," I say, taking a chance and sitting on the edge of her bed. "If I wanted to take your fangs out, I would've done it while you were delirious and told you it was a monster dentist that broke into the dorm."

"That's true," she says, tapping the lid of the vial.

"Seriously?" I ask. "That's what works for you? Not that I have been helping you all this time, but that I didn't actively harm you while you were helpless?"

Tina pops the cap, takes a sniff.

"It means a lot." She shrugs.

"Drink up," I say and give her a hard look.

Whipping her head back, she downs the potion. A second passes, her eyes focus on mine. And then she's up and running, hitting the door of the bathroom so hard that it swings back and smacks me in the face when I try to follow.

"Thanks a lot, roomie!" I yell, rubbing my forehead.

I don't get an answer—not in words, anyway—but a sound comes from the windowsill.

Oh gods.

Apparently Tina's symbiosis with Vee knows no boundaries.

I walk over to the plant and hold my cupped hands below its mouth.

"Go ahead," I say. Vee gives another little cough, and a three half-digested flies drop into my hands.

"Good job, Vee."

I guess this is how I finally make friends with my roommate.

30

W hen you wake up first thing in the morning aware that you're going to murder things, it makes you puke. Actually, it's also the sound of Tina puking that makes me puke. Unfortunately, she's using the bathroom so I have to run to the window, and accidentally spatter a bird-shifter looking for breakfast, who shifts back into human from the shock.

"Sorry," I call, wiping my mouth before I shut the window.

"Tina?" I knock timidly on the bathroom door. A puking vampire must be approached with caution. "You okay in there?"

A grudging, "I'm fine," is all I get from her. She gives no indication of how much longer she's going to be in there. I practically run down the hall to Cassie's room, barely knocking before I barge in to use her bathroom. When I pop back out, I see that she's pulling on a battle pack.

"Whoa, Cassie. What are you doing?"

She pulls her hair up into a ponytail. "I'm coming with you," she says.

There's no way Cassie is up for this. She still isn't fully recovered from what she witnessed when we rescued her from the stronghold, let alone ready to actively participate in...in...whatever it is this raid is supposed to be.

"No, you're not," I tell her. "There's no way Merilee would agree to this."

"I gave my mom the slip," she admits. "I love her but since I've been back all she's done is smother me."

"Can you blame her? You were freaking kidnapped."

"I know...I just need this." She shrugs. "She's hasn't been herself since I returned. First she was worried about the monsters trying to take *me* again. But then the gods told Mom they're now more worried about the monsters taking her. Apparently, the monsters believed Mom was an old crone. Obviously they got some bad intel from someone. Anyway, now they know she's young and won't be dying anytime soon. It's likely if they try again, they'll go straight for her. So the gods are keeping Mom under lock and key, and she's a nervous wreck. Themis is trying to distract her with some project about an old prophecy. That's helping. And today she found something that got her all excited. I figured it was a good chance to slip away, so I told her I needed a change of clothes."

"Your clothes are magic. They change automatically." Merilee must be deep in research to let Cassie out of her sight with such a lame excuse.

I sigh. "Are you sure you want to do this?" I ask her.

"Absolutely." She says it with more steel then I've seen in her since she's been back.

"You'll have to get approval, and I may have used up all my leverage getting Greg on the team."

"Already done. Maddox says I need to toughen up,"

Cassie tells me. "And Nico says nothing gets you past your first murder like the second one."

"Of course he does. Look, Cassie—"

"No! *You* look, Edie!" My friend suddenly whirls on me, anger in her eyes. "You know I've been through every discipline cycle at the Academy. And I've failed every one. The assassin track is my last shot, and I can't succeed if I'm…if I'm…"

She holds out one hand to illustrate. She's shaking like a leaf in the wind. I take it, cradling it in my own.

"And what if you do succeed?" I ask. "What if you go out there and kill a bunch of monsters? You won't be yourself anymore."

"No," she takes her hand back. "But maybe I'll be useful."

———

We walk to the portal in silence, Cassie beside me, her eyes on the ground.

It's early morning, so I don't see Val right away when he emerges from the mist. But I do see Larissa. It's hard to miss her when she materializes right in front of me, grabbing me in a freaky strong vampire hug.

"Aren't you so excited?" she asks me, eyes alight. "Today I go on my first mission for Mount Olympus Academy!"

"Yes, it's…" My eyes go to Val, a bright blush creeping up my face as I struggle to free myself from the arms of his fiancée.

"I'm so glad I am with you, Edie," Larissa says, keeping her hand on my arm as we walk to the portal together. "You were one of my first friends here."

Behind us, there's a stifled giggle.

I turn to see Greg in bat form flitting around behind us. Nico was against Jordan and Greg joining the team but I fought for them. Jordan was a shoo in, even if Nico doesn't like him. He's one of the best spies in the school. Greg was not about to be left behind and I said that if he wasn't going than neither was I. That settled the matter.

"Hey Edie, I bet you never thought you'd be besties with a vamp, huh?" Greg squeaks at me.

"Shut up," I mutter at him, then jerk in surprise when something brushes past my leg. It's Jordan, blitzing through the morning on his panther legs, absolutely ecstatic to be able to shift again.

"You guys! Check me out!" He actually rolls onto his back in front of me, showing off the fully glory of his belly and his...

"Seriously, dude?" I ask.

"Sorry." He snaps back into human form. "I'm very excited."

"Obviously," I say.

"Shifting into panther form is my second favorite thing to do," he says. "The first being..."

"We get it," I tell him.

"Sex," Greg adds. "He was going to say sex."

I roll my eyes and answer Cassie's questioning stare. "They're not saying anything important. If they do, I'll translate," I promise.

"Good to see everyone," Maddox's voice cuts through the morning. She must have already thrown a key through, because the portal is glowing. She stands in front of it, lit from behind, terrifying as all holy Hades. Nico joins her, his face set on what I can only call "murder mode."

Beside me, Cassie stiffens.

"Are they all here?" Maddox asks Nico, and he surveys

his team. Without meaning to, I stand a little straighter as his eyes pass over me, Larissa, Val, Cassie, Greg, Jordan, Hepa, and a handful of other students.

"All present, and ready for action," Nico says.

I hear a slight murmur from Cassie, something I can't pin down.

"Ladies and gentlemen." Maddox's face tightens a little when she spots Val and Larissa in the crowd. She lifts her nose like she just got a whiff of some rotten scent. Her dislike of vampires sticks, even when going into the monsters' den.

"Students and soldiers," she continues. "Today we strike back! Remnants of the cell that attacked the Academy, tortured my son, and kidnapped one of our own beloved seers have amassed in the ruins of an old stone circle. Our intelligence tells me that Falcus himself is there."

I remember Mavis telling me about Falcus—he's the one who killed Darcy!

"We will have the element of surprise on our side," Maddox continues. "But make no mistake—that cannot be our only weapon. You must fight with all that you have— teeth, claws, magic—and fire." Her gaze lands on me. What she said at dinner the other night echoes in my head.

You are with us, or you are our enemy. And death comes to my enemies.

I nod, unable to break eye contact. Maddox gives us all one last hard stare, then passes through the light. Nico follows, and there's practically a rush after that, everyone is so excited to get to killing after Maddox's speech.

I'm rushed along, pushed through the portal by the flow of students—and into instant pandemonium.

Whether they knew we were coming, or Maddox didn't manage to kill the portal guard quick enough—which I doubt—I don't have time to debate. There's a scimitar coming straight for my head, wielded by a wild-eyed gorgon. I manage to avoid eye contact—she could turn me to stone —as I shift.

I come into my dragon form with a fiery roar. My talons take off her head with one swipe.

With a powerful surge of my wings, I take to the air, surveying the situation.

The stone circle is at the top of a hill that gently slopes down into a grassy glen. There's a forest to the west and a valley, but most of the small force of monsters is at the portal. They try to kill our students before they can make it through.

Jordan is dashing between giant standing stones, snagging monsters by the ankles and dragging them out into the light of torches that Hepa is setting around the perimeter. Once all the torches are up, they'll create a magical barrier to keep the monsters from going through our portal. I watch as Hepa sticks another one into the ground and then lights it with her hands. A minotaur makes a run at her, but Jordan deflects it just in time, getting rolled for his trouble— literally by the minotaur, and an eye-roll from Hepa after he yells at her.

"I saved you! I'm your hero! You gotta love me now!"

Even though she probably can't understand all he's saying in shifter form, the tone probably got the thought across.

Val and Larissa are side by side, leaping as one while monsters scatter. Greg is airborne, too, shouting out positions to fellow shifters below.

But there's an organized counterattack going on that Greg doesn't see, flanking him from the west. I swoop down, blasting a protective wall of fire between my friends and the oncoming monsters.

"Gods dammit, Edie!" Nico yells at me, fist in the air. "Stop defending us. We can handle ourselves. Go on the offensive!"

I reel to the east, pretending I didn't hear him. I know he wants me to fry all our enemies, not just use my fire to protect Academy soldiers. But I've still got blood on my hands from the last time, and it doesn't sit well with my conscience.

I'm not the only one airborne. I share the sky with my fellow winged shifters, but also harpies and a few monsters that ride a pegasus. One rider is a minotaur...is that Falcus? He swings a mighty axe as he rides toward the stone circle.

I spy a few shadows slipping into the tree line, a couple of wood nymphs going for the comfort of the trees. I grab them in my claws, giving them a toss into the air. I don't see where they land, and don't know if they fell far enough to be injured. I didn't crush them, couldn't bring myself to do it after feeling their frightened squirming in my claws.

There's a yell below, and I turn to see that one of Hepa's torches has been overturned. A harpy grabs it, launching it at Greg as he flaps around her. But Hepa spelled the fire to only burn monsters, and when Greg wrenches it from her hands and drops it onto her head, the harpy goes up in flames.

Just like Ocypete did.

No, I can't think about that right now. Even Mavis admitted that these monsters—the ones led by Falcus— were bloodthirsty, bent on harming the gods at any costs, even if it meant taking students down to get to them.

An ear-splitting war cry comes from below and I look

down to see Falcus standing in the middle of the stone circle, his pegasus mount dead on the ground. He wields a bloody axe. Maddox paces around him. Beside him crouches a female manticore, a squirming bundle in her arms.

Gods no, not...I land with a crash, sending my fellow students scattering. Quickly, I switch back into human form. Falcus can't be distracted from Maddox, who is taking jabs at him with a long spear, but the female manticore looks up at me, eyes wide.

It's her. It's the mother from the desert stronghold where we rescued Cassie, the one whose baby Cassie delivered. And that means...

I remember her eyes, the crying baby, the way she looked at me as she begged me to spare the minotaur I had just run down—the father of her baby. Falcus.

"No," I say aloud. "No. No. No!"

Maybe Maddox and Nico were right all along. Maybe I should have killed Falcus then, and his wife and child too. Then we wouldn't be here, standing in a ring of fire and stone in the black of night, watching a murderous circus play out.

All around me, students are injured. Jordan is licking a deep gash on his paw, and Greg has shifted into human form, one arm at an impossible angle. There's a vampire leaking black blood from her side as she lies on the ground, while Hepa, calm yet urgent, says incantations over her.

I can't help but tally the monster count, too. A headless gorgon—my kill, I remember. The battered body of a chimera, fur matted with blood. The charred body of the harpy and the broken manticore, hanging lifeless from the top of a stone pillar. Nymphs, giant scorpions, centaurs.

All lie dead on the battlefield.

31

Any of the other monsters that are not too wounded to run have fled.

Except for Falcus and his family.

The students form a circle to watch the final fight.

"Stop," I say.

It's quiet, and doesn't come out with any force, or fire. I'm exhausted, physically and emotionally. I drop to my knees, and suddenly Cassie is by my side.

"Edie," she says. "Edie, you've got to stay with me. I need your help."

"Are you injured?" I ask, desperately afraid for her.

"No, I need your help with them." Her voice is so clear and powerful. Where is she finding her strength?

I open my eyes, and see her own wide ones, not far from mine. She's looking at the manticore—Falcus' wife—and the baby. She doesn't look scared. She isn't shaking. And suddenly I understand. That's why Cassie is here. That's what she meant about finally being useful.

Cassie is going to save the baby she delivered.

But not if Maddox has anything to do with it. Falcus is

failing fast, one arm bloodied and dangling, the other swinging the axe in deadly arcs...but not quickly enough.

Nico, in wolf form, is dodging in and out, taking bites from the minotaur's muscular legs, while Maddox gracefully dodges out of the circular swings of his axe, her spear arcing in and just grazing Falcus' ribs with every jab.

"They're playing with him," a voice says, and I look up to find that Val is at my other side. He grips my elbow, pulling me to my feet.

"This isn't right," I say, breathlessly, just as Nico feints to the left, then nips Falcus' heel.

The minotaur roars in rage and spins to face Nico, only to have Maddox's spear take one of his ears off. Reeling again, he turns to face her—and Nico makes his move. With the father distracted, Nico grabs the baby from the mother's arms and darts into the crowd of students.

The manticore screams, and Falcus wheels again, ready to protect her—and his child.

Gods and monsters aren't all that different from us, I remember Mavis telling me. *They have enemies and old feuds and good friends...and they fall in love.*

Love. These aren't monsters facing down students in a war. This is a father protecting his wife and child—outnumbered by tormentors.

"Stop!" I say again, louder this time. I am yet again ignored.

Maddox runs her spear through the minotaur's meaty upper arm, and he loses his grip on the axe. Maddox plucks it from the air and delivers one quick swing. Falcus' head spins off into the night, his blood spraying onto the upturned face of his wife.

There are cries among the students—some of them in victorious celebration, but more than a few sound horrified.

There's a sharp wail and I turn to see Cassie has wrestled Nico to the ground, her anger stunning him, his unwillingness to hurt her giving her the advantage as she tears the monster baby from his arms.

"My baby!" The manticore screams, still on her hands and knees. And then Maddox drives the axe downward, slicing the mother's head in two. Everything goes quiet, and Maddox stalks out from inside the stone circle to face Cassie.

"Give that thing to me," she says, one blood-covered hand held out to Cassie.

"No," Cassie says, holding the bundle close. "You can't have it."

"Listen, *seer*," Maddox says. "You're lucky we even let your dead weight along on this ride."

"Lucky?!" Cassie scoffs. "Yes, I'm so fortunate to have witnessed this massacre." She waves her free arm around, taking in the toppled torches, the wounded students, and the dead monsters. "This isn't war, Maddox." she says. "And you're no solider. This is a pillage, and *you're* the monster."

There are a few gasps, and Nico rolls onto his feet, a low warning growl in his throat.

"Vampire," Maddox says, directing her words at Larissa. "Restrain the traitor."

"I am, how do you say, sorry?" Larissa says in an exaggerated accent. "I do not understand you, as English is not my original language." She smiles as she steps in front of Cassie. I want to hug her for her loyalty.

"Don't hide behind your ignorance." Maddox steps forward, axe aloft. "Oh Hades, I'll take you both down with that squalling thing, then," she says, with a shrug. "You certainly won't be the first vampire I've killed."

Across the circle of students, Val bristles as well.

Maddox tosses the axe at Cassie's feet then shifts into her wolf form. She's horrifying, large and sleek, dark as the night around us.

"Last chance, seer," she growls at Cassie. "Drop the baby."

"No," Cassie says, "Make love, not war."

She's shaking and I see her color fading as Maddox advances. I shift, although it takes all my energy, and fold my wings around her. But Cassie looks up at me, meeting my dragon's eyes. She shakes her head and then turns forward and purposely steps beyond the shelter of my wings.

I realize she doesn't want me to protect her. Not this time. She needs to stand up for what she feels is right, find the purpose that has eluded her at the Academy for so long.

Still I stay in dragon form, in case she needs me.

Another growl joins Maddox's, but it's different, higher, almost like a question. Between Cassie and his mother Nico paces, looking undecidedly between them.

Maddox crouches lower, ears laid back, leg muscles bunching. She howls up at the sky. I feel it down the length of my long curving spine.

There are several answering howls and I whip my head towards them just in time to see three werewolves attack Val. He falls beneath them and disappears.

"Val!" Larissa cries.

Despite his injuries, Jordan is the first to jump into the fray. I'm not far behind.

I grab one of the wolves by the scruff of his neck and lift a few feet of the ground. The coward immediately begins to whine pitifully. Remembering he's a fellow student, I pitch him towards the ground like he's a bowling ball. Predictably he rolls several times before coming to a stop on his back.

Planting two claws on his chest with my talons resting what I hope is uncomfortably close to his belly, I screech at him.

"What do you think you're doing?"

The smell of urine fills the air and I realize he's peed himself. Whimpering, he tells me, "Maddox told us to. When she gave the signal—go for Val."

I rise into the air and whirl around, my heart in my mouth.

I see Cassie running toward the portal, the wailing of the baby manticore trailing in her wake.

Behind her Larissa and Hepa work together blocking Callie from Maddox. Hepa throws balls of fire from her hands.

Pop. Pop. Pop.

One after another they hit Maddox. They don't seem to slow her down much, but at least they're a distraction. And they seem to throw off her sense a little, allowing Larissa to get in close and do some damage.

Larissa may be small and dainty, but she is a vampire. I've never seen her fangs—she always keeps them politely hidden. But now her deadly vampire nature is on full display.

I watch Cassie disappear through the portal at the same time that Larissa comes at Maddox again. But this time Maddox is waiting for her.

Larissa screams as Maddox's teeth close around her shoulder. She claws at Maddox, her fangs useless, but she still has her vampire strength—enough to pull out great fistfuls of fur.

Still, Larissa isn't looking good as Maddox gets her on the ground, with a giant paw over her chest.

I am already in the air, wings parallel to the ground for maximum speed.

But it's too late.

There's a sudden, sharp crack, and I when I look back I see Maddox sprawling over Larissa's body, her neck at an odd angle, the light gone from her eyes.

Larissa is dead.

32

"No!" I screech. Hitting the ground hard, I shift back into human form. The baby's blanket is at my feet and I grab it, then bundle it up, hoping everyone will think I now have the baby.

Hoping to buy Cassie some time.

"Jordan, go with Cassie!" I yell at him, and he's off after her, running awkwardly on three legs, but still fast.

Hepa runs toward the portal too—with Maddox on her heels.

I dig deep, ready to shift again, when a bolt of lightning comes out of the clear sky and strikes inches from Maddox's nose. Maddox yelps. Then swivels her head in all directions.

"Zee?" she barks.

But that lightning bolt didn't come from Zee.

I turn to Val in time to see him throw aside the limp body of the werewolf that had been attacking him. They're both covered in blood. But Val is the one who's still standing.

I clutch the empty blanket to my chest as Val makes his way to Larissa's broken body. Obviously hurting, he moves slowly. Reaching Larissa, he falls to his knees and then leans over her, quietly touching her face. He's shaking, silently, as tears of blood drip down his face and splatter Larissa's pale skin.

Maddox lets loose a guttural growl then shifts back into her human form. There is silence in the stone circle, as the remaining students look at one another, in shock. We just saw a teacher murder a student.

Even Nico, who has also shifted, looks lost. He turns to the wolves who attacked Val. "What is wrong with you?" I think it's what he wants to say to his mom...but can't.

Finally, Maddox speaks. "Calm down, Nico. They were just following orders."

He looks astonished. "I didn't give that order."

"No, I did." Maddox says. And then she turns her back on her son, dismissing him. I freeze at she focuses in on me instead. "I told you, Edie. You are with me, or you are my enemy. And death comes to my enemies." She spits Larissa's vampire blood from her mouth. "It is time for you to choose." She eyes the bundle in my arms.

"Edie, don't," Greg shouts weakly, but I silence him with a look.

I rise up on my wings, a glorious fire red, and shift fully into my dragon form, my spiked spine tearing out of my back as I throw the bundle into the air. Some of the students below me gasp as I let loose a ball of flame that incinerates the bundle in midair, leaving only ashes to fall in their upturned faces.

I descend, landing before Maddox. Her battle glazed eyes are gleeful. "I thought you were a good choice for my son. You are worthy of him. But now I'm not sure if he's worthy of you."

I shift into my human form and look her in the eyes.

"Everyone at the Academy will know what happened here today," I promise.

She takes my proclamation as praise, giving me a quick squeeze on the shoulder.

"Nico," Maddox says. "Have you forgotten you're leading this mission?"

"Really? I get to lead it now?" Poor Nico. He looks devastated and furious all at once. "Maddox, you're dismissed. Get out of here."

Her eyes go wide. "You don't speak to me that way."

"I don't want to speak to you at all." This time it's Nico who turns his back on Maddox. She stares at him for a long moment. Momentarily bewildered, but then quickly hardening again.

Head high, shoulders back, she stalks to the portal and is gone.

Nico watches her and after she disappears, he continues looking at the spot where she last stood, until finally shaking himself out of it and returning to business.

"Trackers, make sure all the monsters have been killed," he snaps. "Witches and warlocks, maintain the perimeter." He looks at Val, still weeping over Larissa's body. "Vampire, bring the Academy dead back through the portal. They will be buried with honors."

I take a step forward. "I'll take Larissa."

I don't wait for his acknowledgement. I kneel next to Val.

His shirt and pants are torn and deep bite marks ooze blood. Maddox intended for Val to be dead too. This wasn't a heat of the moment thing; it was pre-meditated.

"Let's get her back," I say.

He looks up at me and nods. His tears are gone, only the bloody streaks remain. His face is hard, free of his customary smirk.

Larissa was his intended bride, a beautiful vampire that I should have hated on sight. Instead we became friends. She died defending Cassie, and a helpless baby.

And what did Val and I do? We made out behind her back. At least there is one last thing we can do for her, a debt that we owe.

Together we carry her body through the portal.

———

M y first stop is to the infirmary with Val, where we place Larissa's body in the care of Fern. She is laid out with the rest of the dead.

"I have to talk to her family," Val says. "They trusted me to take care of her."

"Larissa was strong," I assure him, putting a hand on his arm. "She knew what she was doing. She knew that she was sacrificing herself." I can barely believe she's gone. "You did take care of her at the Academy. She loved it here. But you couldn't have stopped her. The choice was hers."

Val looks at me like I'm an idiot. It's an expression I'm used to seeing from Tina. But not him. "I was entrusted with her care and safety. No one will care to hear my excuses. I wouldn't give them regardless. Larissa should never have gone today. But I—" He stops and shakes his head, the tension practically radiating out from his body. "I wanted to be there for you." Disgust twists his face. "And Larissa felt it her duty to stay at my side. So she could have my back."

I don't know what to say to this, and I'm pretty sure anything I do say will only make Val more upset. So we both stay silent, watching as more of the dead students are brought in.

We didn't lose many, but even one is too much. And it's

not like I can forget that not all of the Academy dead were killed by monsters. One of us was killed by our own. As if following my thoughts, Val looks back at Larissa, his mouth a flat, angry line.

"I have to go," I tell Val. "There are things I need to do."

"Like finding out what Cassie did with the baby?" he asks.

My eyes flash up to his. "You know…"

"I know you wouldn't roast a defenseless newborn, even if it is a monster."

"You won't tell?" I ask, though I know the answer.

"Larissa died for that child," he reminds me coldly. "And Cassie too. She protected them from that—" He cuts off and spins to push his fist through the infirmary wall. The exterior is stone from the beginning of time and yet Val created a hole that I can see straight through to the outside.

"I'm going to take care of Maddox," I assure him.

He looks at me, eyes intense. Not alive like Nico's get, but flat. Deadly. "Not if I do it first."

"Val, don't do anything stupid," I warn.

He turns away from me. "I thought you wanted to find Cassie."

Silently, I watch as he sits on a chair beside where Larissa is laid out. He picks up her hand and holds it between two of his own.

My heart breaks. For him. For Larissa. And yes, I'm ashamed to admit it—for me too.

Unable to watch anymore, I spin away and hurry out of the infirmary.

I need to find Cassie, but I decide to go to Themis first—before WWIII breaks out on this campus.

I'm approaching her office door when it bursts open,

Themis nearly taking it off the hinges as she erupts into the hallway, Hepa fast on her heels.

There is a fire in Themis' eyes that I have never seen, before—a good reminder that this isn't just the guidance counselor. She is a goddess, after all.

"This will not stand," Themis says, as she brushes past me in the hallway.

Hepa turns to me, shaking her head. "I had to turn Maddox in. And those werewolves as well. It's not right what Maddox did. Murdering Larissa. Trying to kill a baby. None of this Moggy bullshit is right, either."

"I'm glad you feel that way," I tell her. I'd wondered if her cooled feelings toward Jordan had something to do with Zee's proclamation.

"What? I may be bitchy, but I'm not a bigot."

I laugh, despite myself. "You're not..." but I can't finish. I laugh again. "You're just you. And..." I pause, wondering how many people I can trust with my own secret. It turns out no-bullshit Hepa is the perfect person to tell as I fill her in on how I tricked Maddox with the baby blanket.

"Smart," she nods. "And Mad Maddox bought that?"

"Yeah, she thinks the baby is dead. Where actually is...?" I ask Hepa.

"Cassie wanted to hide the baby in her dorm room, but I told her that was idiotic. I had Jordan take it to his. Figured that was safer, since Greg is his roommate. The little bugger is actually really freaking cute. Fern has been bringing us a potion that has the same properties as manticore milk."

Ugh. Well, that's sort of gross, but I guess it's a good thing. "We just need to keep the baby safe until we can send it back to the monsters. I may know someone who can help us with that."

"Who?" Hepa asks, her gaze intense.

"Just a contact," I tell her vaguely.

"Well, you'd better get in touch with them. If Maddox sniffs out that baby we're all dead."

"She won't," I tell her. "And by the look on Themis' face, she won't be around long enough to catch the scent."

33

We're all sent from our morning classes to the outdoor amphitheater for an Academy-wide meeting. There's some grumbling from Priapus as he makes his way down the wooded path, and a stifled groan every time his wheelbarrow hits a tree root.

Cassie and Fern settle in on either side of me as we find a seat, and I sneak a glance at Val. But he's on the far side of the theatre, deep in conversation with some other vamps. Their eyes are dark, their voices a low rumble, a few fangs erupt as their voices raise in argument.

It makes me nervous watching them. Tensions are at an all-time high and I've got a feeling those vampires—including Val—probably aren't arguing over ways they can help bring everyone together again.

As Themis takes the stage, I do a quick check for Nico. I haven't seen him since the raid. After checking in with Cassie, I came back to my room to find Tina feeling much better...well enough to yell at me for not putting Vee's vomit back into her soil for the extra nutrients.

It had fallen on me to tell Tina that Larissa was dead,

and I'd been surprised to see some blood tears well in her eyes. Vee hung her head too, leaves drooping, when Tina left. She didn't come back to the dorm until halfway through the night.

But Nico I haven't seen...and he's not here in the amphitheater now. I wonder if he's patched things up with his mom. I really hope he hasn't.

"Attention, everyone," Themis says, her voice immediately settling the students. Mr. Zee and Hermes are sitting in chairs on the dais, Mr. Zee staring moodily at his feet as Themis makes her announcement.

"As I'm sure you're all aware, Mount Olympus Academy sent in a tactical strike team yesterday to eliminate the last of the monster cell that kidnapped one of our students and tortured another."

There are some claps and cheers from the crowd, as some students do what they think Themis wants—applaud the death of monsters. But she raises her hand for quiet, and everyone settles again.

"And while the actions of the monsters are inexcusable, I'm sorry to say it has come to our attention that other atrocities occurred yesterday." There's a low murmur, but Themis continues.

"War is ugly, no one can argue against that. But who do we become if we sink to the level of our opponent? How can we claim to be superior to our enemy if we employ their own tactics? We fight for glory and we do it with honor."

There's a smattering of applause.

"We do not send a plague to do our fighting for us," Themis says, her voice rising.

There's a rumble of agreement from the students.

"We do not drag a defenseless seer from her bed in the night," Themis cries.

Shouts answer her, the benches growing more agitated now.

"We do not murder children in their mother's arms," Themis says, her voice now low, dull. Threatening. "And we do not encourage—no, *order*—students to attack another student."

She's met with silence, students looking at one another questioningly, unsure how they are supposed to respond.

"No!" Themis shakes her head. "*We* do not. Unfortunately, someone who was entrusted with your education"— she shoots a dark glance at Mr. Zee, but he's staring at the floor between his feet— "has taken it upon themselves to behave in a manner that is unbecoming to the Academy. Bring her in!"

Behind Themis, Kratos emerges from between two pillars, barely able to hide his delight as he leads Maddox by the elbow. Her head is high, even when Themis matches her gaze. Maddox scans the crowd, and some students sit down quickly, as if afraid to be caught participating in her downfall.

"I have done nothing wrong," Maddox says, her voice loud and carrying. "I am a werewolf and a warrior, and I fight for what I believe in," she declares, baring her teeth.

"You killed a vampire!" someone shouts from behind me, and general agreement rises from the crowd, along with a low, gathered hissing from fellow vamps.

"And I'd do it again," Maddox shouts back. The hissing rises in intensity.

"Enough!" Themis shouts, her booming voice shutting down both the students and Maddox. After Maddox has settled, the three werewolves who attacked Val file in behind her, heads down, feet dragging.

"These students," Themis says, indicating the werewolves, "attacked another student. This is against the student code of conduct and would normally result in expulsion. However, as they were only following orders from supervising faculty, they will only be on probation."

With this the werewolves are dismissed, and Themis turns her attention to Maddox.

"Maddox Tralano, for war crimes, and fatal assault upon a student of the Academy, you are hereby dismissed from your position and banished from Mount Olympus Academy."

The hissing is back. Louder, this time.

"Fired!?" someone shouts. "She murdered one of us and all you do is fire her?"

There are some murmurs of agreement, but most of the students are bewildered, looking back and forth between Themis and Maddox, unsure who to believe, or who to follow.

Themis nods, as if in agreement with whoever shouted. "For her crimes, Maddox Tralano is expelled from school grounds, and a dose of the shifting plague will be forcefully administered to her."

Maddox reacts violently to this, fighting against Kratos' grip. He has her tight, and though Maddox is a frightening creature in her own right, Kratos is a god. He has to hold her as Themis reads out her sentence.

"Maddox Tralano," Themis declares. "You will be rendered human."

———

A few days later, during Maddox's usual class time, I instead visit the future site of the Larissa Golov memorial building for sexual health and information. I guess her parents wanted to make sure she'd always be remembered. In her letters home she'd raved about Priapus' class and how much she was learning. So now, thanks to a generous donation made in Larissa's name, he'll now have a permanent place on campus to misinform students.

It's a sweet, odd, and unintentionally hilarious tribute. Just like Larissa—it's perfect.

"Priapus really pushed for a big old bus too, so he could spread his knowledge around the world," says a voice in my ear. "Thankfully, the Golovs thought that was a bit much and shot it down."

"Val," I say, turning to him. "How are you doing?"

I'm a little nervous seeing him again after he was in such a dark place after Larissa's death. But now he's wearing one of his usual T-shirts. Today's has a half-eaten fortune cookie with a fortune that reads, *This cookie is poisoned*. The nearly radioactive tension that surrounded him last time is gone too.

Which seems...fast.

In answer to my question, he gives a half shrug. "Larissa is dead. And yet life goes on. It feels like it shouldn't, or like everything should feel different. But it isn't. I wake up, drink blood, go to class. It's all the same as always, and yet...not."

I nod, understanding completely. I felt the same way after losing my dad.

"I'm sorry, Val."

This earns another shrug. But then he reaches out and takes hold of my hand. We stand side by side, fingers linked, studying the empty space that will soon be Larissa's memorial. I think of all I've lost, but of all I've gained, too. My friends. My dragon. My sister returned to me.

Life does go on. And I've found a way to go with it.

I lean my head against Val's shoulder, feeling lighter. Almost at peace.

The dangerous monster faction is gone. Sure there's still a war going on, but that's been the case for centuries. Maybe now, though, it will go back to being more of a cold war with spy games and tracking, but no battles. No killing.

Val's lips brush the top of my head.

I slowly turn, lifting my face to his.

This could be my happy ending, I think.

And then the screaming starts.

34

Val and I rush towards the quad, following the sounds of screams. Hand in hand, we pass the spot where Jenn Lamont's ashes were found, and I shudder, fighting a sudden rush of *déjà vu*. But this time it's not the embers of a vampire that has brought shocked students out to see what has happened. It's Nico carrying a corpse.

And not just any corpse—Nico is carrying his mother.

He lowers her body to the ground, the face still recognizable even though it's bloated. Nico is in shock, stuck halfway through a shift. His teeth are long when his eye locks on mine in the crowd.

"Edie...she's dead."

I step forward, I can't help but react to his pleading, desperate eye.

"Themis kept me for questioning after the mission," he goes on. "They didn't tell me what happened until after they'd banished her. They didn't even let me say goodbye."

He stumbles toward me, weak as the day I found him in the desert. But this time it's not physical wounds that have harmed him. Nico is hurting on the inside, and he doesn't know how to handle it. He holds on to me like I'm the only other person in the quad, though we're surrounded by most of the school.

"I tried to follow her scent through the swamp," he says, sobbing into my shoulder. "I couldn't just let her go like that. I wanted to say goodbye. But I couldn't..." He takes a deep breath. "It was so hard to find her smell, since now she's..." he shudders. "Human."

"What happened?" I ask, wiping tears from his cheeks.

"I finally found her trail, followed her as best I could. I came across a place where there were sure signs of a struggle. And she was there...dumped in the swamp like a piece of trash!" he spits out the word. Finally, he notices the crowd around him. "Which one of you bloodsuckers did this?" he asks.

"She deserved it!" someone shouts and Nico whirls.

"You wait until she's defenseless and alone—then you attack! You don't have an ounce of honor."

"*She* had no honor," Val says from behind me, and I turn, Nico pressing up against me from behind as he lunges at Val.

"What has happened now?" Themis asks, bursting through the crowd.

"This is all *your* fault!" Nico shouts, shifting and leaping for Themis' throat. In one motion Themis reaches out her hand, grabs him by the scruff of the neck and holds him to the ground. He howls and struggles, and when he can't break loose, shifts back into human form.

"You hated her," he yells from the ground, even though Themis is practically crushing his windpipe. "You hated how good she was. This is all your fault," he repeats.

"Maddox has no one to blame for this but herself,"

Themis says quietly. Her eyes scan the crowd and rest on Hepa where she stands with Jordan. "Hepa, bring me a sedative. The strongest we have."

Hepa nods and hurries off. Themis once again turns her attention to Nico. "Your mother loved the Academy, but it was a sick love." She tells him. "You must cut out a sickness."

Hepa returns with the sedative and Themis holds it above Nico's struggling form. "Are you a sickness, Nico?"

Her eyes flash and he stops struggling. She holds the vial to his mouth and he drinks. Almost immediately his body sags. A moment later his eyes slide closed.

Themis stands over Nico's unconscious body, waiting until his tongue lolls out the side of his mouth before turning to the rest of us.

"Everyone, back to what you were doing."

Despite her words, no one leaves. We all stand there watching as Themis and some healers carry Nico and his mother's corpse away.

I turn to Val, burying my face in his chest. "This is terrible!" I sob. "Maddox was insane but she didn't deserve to be murdered! Who would just…?" But Val's arms aren't around me. He's not giving me any comfort, and his body is rigid.

"No," I say, backing away, hoping he'll tell me I'm wrong. Hoping he'll stop my racing thoughts.

"It was for Larissa," he says the words without inflection.

"You…you…" I don't have words for him. Suddenly I realize why his mood changed so drastically. He killed Maddox. That made him feel better. Not awful. Not torn over taking someone else's life.

Life goes on, he said. But because of him, Maddox's won't.

"Stay away from me," I tell him, following the trail of healers to the infirmary, my thoughts a mixed jumble.

Yes, Maddox killed in cold blood. Maybe there is some justice is doing the same to her. An eye for an eye. Isn't that what I wanted when I came to MOA? Revenge?

I don't want that anymore, I realize. If we all keep killing to even the score—where does it ever end? All my hunger to kill monsters and avenge my family somehow disappeared when I wasn't looking.

———

I am with Nico when he wakes.

"I'm so sorry..." I start but he shakes his head.

"You've done nothing wrong, Edie."

"What will *you* do?" I ask. Behind us, Fern cleans up the table where some vials have overturned. I lower my voice. "You can't attack Themis again. That was foolish."

I don't remind him it was futile. She swatted him out of the air like a mosquito.

"I'll stay at the Academy," he says. "Help Zeus. Keep an eye on Themis. My mother wouldn't have run away and neither will I."

"Please don't..." What do I say? Please don't kill Val, even though he probably murdered your mom? "Make the divisions among the students any worse," I finish lamely. "I know you're upset about your mother, but the guilty will be punished."

He reaches out and grabs my hand. "If you're with me, Edie, I think I can control myself."

"That's a lot to put on someone," Fern says.

Nico growls at her. "No one asked your opinion, witch. This is between me and Edie." He sits up, takes my other hand. "My mother approved of you. She wanted us to be together. After you killed the baby on the field of battle, I knew you were on the right side, finally. There's a place for violence and bloodlust, Edie. I think you know that now. And the best way to honor my mother's memory is to do what she wanted. Edie, will you be mine?"

The room is closing in on me. I think I was just proposed to by a one-eyed werewolf who my sister tried to kill, and whose mother my kind-of-vampire-boyfriend murdered, after she, in turn, murdered his fiancée.

What am I supposed to say?

If I say *no*, will Nico go on a killing spree?

If I say yes...well, by the look on Nico's face, if I say yes, we'll be consummating that decision right here in the infirmary.

"Can I have some time?" I ask and his face grows stormy. "Emotions are high right now," I clarify. "I want to focus on my work at the Academy. I need to graduate from the assassination class." At least that's something he understands.

Fern tries to save me. "Edie, I need to speak with you about something."

I look down at Nico. "We'll talk later. Just...if you feel like killing someone...please don't."

He nods, which is as good an affirmation as I can hope for.

Fern takes me outside and we walk in one of the gardens. "Edie, I've been talking to my contacts about our little bundle of joy."

"And...?"

"We have a home for her. If you take her to"—she looks around to make sure we're alone—"the *island*, someone will be waiting there for you."

"You knew all along?" I ask. "That Mavis was Emmie and where she was?"

Fern swallows. "I'm still working to help the monsters.

And so are you...whether you mean to or not. You aligned yourself with the monsters and became a traitor to the Academy the moment you saved that baby. Bringing her to them is treason. Everyone involved could be banished—or worse. Do you understand what I'm saying?"

Her eyes narrow at me and I do. She doesn't just mean me. She means Cassie and Jordan and Greg and Hepa, too.

"It's the right thing to do," I tell her.

Fern nods. "I don't want students to die. I don't want monsters to die. I want peace."

"Is it possible?"

"If we work together. Will you work with us?"

"I'll get the baby to the island," I tell her, not fully answering. "When?"

"Tomorrow. Can you keep her secret until then?"

"The history of my entire life was kept a secret from me until I was seventeen. I'm pretty sure I can keep my mouth shut for twenty-four hours," I tell her.

———

I might be able to keep my mouth shut, but keeping a baby manticore's mouth shut is a totally different thing.

"Oh my gods," Jordan says, holding the wailing baby three feet in the air as pee dribbles out of it. "It doesn't stop making noise and it doesn't stop making messes."

"It's a baby," Cassie reminds him, wrapping the wriggling monster into a fresh blanket while she coos at it. It immediately settles, and a scorpion tail pops out of the bundle to boop her nose.

"Awwww...." Cassie smiles at me, her good humor completely restored. "I think she likes me."

"I think two weeks from now that same move will take your nose right off your face," Greg says, as he shakes a vial.

"What's that?" I ask.

"Manticore milk potion, I guess?" he says. "Fern says I have to shake it and it will self-heat to the right temperature for a manticore baby which is—"

"Pretty gods-damned hot," Jordan says, holding out his forearm to show me a burn on his wrist. "I was checking it to make sure it was the right temperature like we do for bottle-fed kittens at home, and it gave me a second-degree burn."

"Baby didn't mind though, did you?" Cassie says, popping the bottle in its mouth and switching to baby talk. "You took it right out of Jordan's hands and got down to business, didn't you?"

"Well, that's kind of what I'm worried about," Greg says. "What if her next order of business is eating something that tastes like shifter?"

"She wouldn't!" Cassie snaps, glaring up at him from the baby.

"Cassie," I say quietly, "she might. None of us have any experience raising babies, let alone a monster baby. And we can't risk being caught in the dorms with her, either. You know she'd be killed if she was found, and all of us punished."

Cassie turns her head back to the baby and begins to sway her arms, humming softly.

"Cassie, you did a noble thing, but don't make your sacrifice meaningless," I say, crossing the room to stand next to her. I peer down into the blanket, expecting to see something hideous. Instead, I see that Hepa was right. The manticore baby is adorable.

She's like an overgrown kitten, her little wings pressed against her back, scorpion tail wrapped around her front paws, glowing leonine eyes locked on Cassie's as she drinks from the bottle.

"Oh my gods, she's cute," I say, entranced.

"I know, I know," Cassie says, with glee. "I just want to rub her wittle belly," Cassie says, snuggling one hand into the bundle. The baby starts to purr.

"Okay, okay," I say. "But we still have to get her back to her people."

"I know we do," Cassie says, still rocking the baby. "Eventually."

"Eventually, as in tomorrow," I tell her.

"What?" everyone asks.

I hold my arms out, and Cassie hands over the baby reluctantly. It's warm and solid in my arms, the golden eyes locking onto mine.

"I hope you like flying," I tell her.

35

The baby sleeps in my arms as I stand on shore, waiting for Mavis. It's small and helpless, yet so sweet and warm at the same time. The manticore had cuddled against me when we passed through the portal, then nuzzled my chest, purring as I shifted and flew us to the island.

How can anyone hate this tiny baby?

A cat runs toward me on the sand, brushes against my legs, then walks away, beckoning me to follow. Mavis leads me to a small boat, crewed by a trio of manticores. One jumps down and stalks toward me, its scorpion's tail flicking from side to side.

"You're the one who saved my niece?" she asks, her face filled with hope.

"I am." I hand her the baby. She sits the baby on her lap to give her a quick examination.

"She looks happy and well-fed. Thank you," she says, looking away from the baby now held close to her chest. "Thank you for your kindness."

Mavis shifts, hugs the manticores and we watch them

sail away.

I hope that baby is safe. I hope she never has to fight in this war.

"You did a good thing," Mavis tells me. "But you could do more good. Those monsters you just met, those are the ones I've aligned myself with. Falcus and his crew were bloodthirsty. The monsters I know and love only want peace. What do you want, Edie?" Her question hangs in the air.

I hesitate, wanting to make sure I'm making the right decision. "Seeing all the hate at the Academy and how easily Maddox riled everyone up with just a few speeches...it was awful. And eye-opening. I want to be on the right side." I sigh. "So I guess that means I'm with you."

She turns to me, arms open, a huge smile on her face.

"No killing," I say firmly, one hand out to stop the hug. "Rescue and reconnaissance only."

She pushes my arm out of the way, going in for a squeeze. "This is great. I'll move to Athens and be your handler. There's so much we can do together."

We walk along the beach for a while and up to her cave. It's dark inside and it takes me a moment for my eyes to adjust, but Mavis doesn't have that problem; her cat-eyes scan the inside, alerting her to danger. She grabs my wrist.

"Someone's been here," she says, seconds before a figure blocks the exit.

"Been knocked down a few pegs in the world, haven't you?" A familiar voice says.

"From Academy darling to cave-woman," Nico says, cutting the distance between us with a few strides. "How far you've fallen, Emmie."

He draws her name out, like he's tasting it.

"Or should I say...Mavis?"

THERE'S MORE TO READ IN THE MYTHVERSE...

Want to know about all the latest releases? Sign up for the Mythverse Newsletter!

When you sign up you'll receive THREE FREE SHORT STORIES—all set in the Mythverse!

If you enjoyed this book please leave a review! It helps us to write more books that our readers will love!

We'd also love to have you join our Facebook group—Mythverse Fandom.

Here you can yell at us about cliffhangers, chat with other fans about the Mythverse, get exclusive early book excerpts, and even snippets from our Slack convos!

———

Keep reading the Mythverse books. The entire series thus far is:

Fire & Flood: Mount Olympus Academy
Pillage & Plague: Mount Olympus Academy
Wither & Wound: Mount Olympus Academy
Amazon Princess: Amazon Academy (with bonus book
CHAOS & CHRISTMAS, A Mount Olympus Academy
Christmas Carol)
Amazon Queen: Amazon Academy
Squad Goals: Underworld Academy
Dream Team: Underworld Academy (coming June 23rd)

———

This fall, get DOWN & DIRTY with our new series! We'll see the Mythverse from the perspective of a human with no superpowers as she tries to navigate a new world full of supernatural creatures.

Thankfully, Nico, your favorite newly reformed one-eyed werewolf, will be around to help her - whether she wants his help or not!

Make sure to pre-order for September 1st 2020, GRAVE NEW WORLD: Down & Dirty Supernatural Cleaning Services

———

Keep reading for a sneak peak at Chapter 1 of Amazon Princess...

CHAPTER ONE

I am beauty, I am grace. I will punch you in the face.

This has become my new mantra since the end of the world. My old mantra was, *Miss Teen Wisconsin or Bust*, but sometimes ya gotta adjust your goals.

I get out of my beat-to-crap pick-up truck carefully, making sure not to step on the train of my long sparkling gown. Even though there aren't any more pageants, I still don't wanna ruin it. All the Swarovski crystals on it cost me an arm and a leg.

Cost me an arm and a leg. That's kinda a joke, but also kinda *not*.

Last week, I totally saw Miss Teen Dairy Queen on the side of the road. She was missing her left leg and had clearly bled out. I tried real hard to *not* think about how that might've happened. Years ago she'd had those long legs insured for something like a hundred grand a piece.

Seems unfair the insurance won't be paying out on them suckers. But a lotta things ain't fair these days, and I can't say it was always all that better in the before times either.

I covered what was left of Desirae up with a blanket. And then, even though I'm not much for religion, I had a little chat with God after I got her all tucked in.

"Hey God, sorry I been cursing your name so much lately. Don't take it personal, okay? I know you get touchy 'bout how folks use your name. But this ain't about me. I'm calling up to you about Desirae here. Dessie was crowned Miss Teen Dairy Queen three years running. Those cow folks loved her legs. Anyway, you treat her like royalty up there, cuz that's what she is."

Who can say whether God was listening? From what I hear 'round town, his response rate isn't what it used to be.

Now, kicking my truck door shut with a combat-booted heel, and clutching my baseball bat, I head into the Piggly Wiggly.

Six months ago, I was Brandee Jean Mason, resident Beauty Queen. Headed for big things and the bright lights... or at least, the state fair circuit.

Then came the earthquakes.

And the floods.

NYC fell into the ocean. California is now an island.

I mean, that's the last I heard.

There hasn't been a news broadcast in months, and the one guy in town who's got a shortwave radio isn't inclined to share info unless I do some sharing of *other* things—and that sure ain't happening. No way, no how.

I think I'd rather not know, anyway.

Now I grab a shopping cart and wipe down the handle with the wet wipes, still in the dispenser. The apocalypse is not a good time to get salmonella.

Wisconsin weathered the storms better than most states. We've got our own farms and fields, and enough people got solar panels and even their own wind turbines, that some folks even still have electric. But unless you know how to hunt, raise, or grow your own food, you're still stuck shopping.

Which can be a real pain in my ass—my very nice, award-winning ass.

Carl looks up from the year-old magazine he's reading behind the check-out line. "Hi, Brandee Jean."

There's a machine gun next to him on the counter. Bandits killed his dad a few months back and he's not about to let them get him too.

I relax a little. Carl's a good guy, always polite. I've known him since middle school.

I push the cart over to him, putting a little swing into my hips. "What we got today?"

"Corn. And more corn." He peeks at me over the magazine. "Nice dress."

"It's my armor." I tell him, doing a twirl, then a little curtsy.

"The baseball bat really makes the outfit. I give it ten out of ten."

My bat is spangled and painted bright red. I found it at the back of my closet, leftover from a "Damn Yankees" dance routine I did years ago. Weaponry is the to-die-for accessory this season, and I do like to stay on trend.

I smile with a wide-open mouth, showing all my teeth, just like I would on the pageant stage. I put a hand to my chest. "Why thank you. I'm just so very honored to be here today."

He laughs. "We did get in a fresh batch of Quik Powder…"

"Well, why didn't you start with that?" I ask.

Quik Powder is a refined food source. You can make bread or pancakes, or just mix it with water and drink it. It tastes like glue, but it also sticks to your ribs in about the same way, which means that you can eat a little and stay full for a whole day.

I load up my cart with five canisters of powder, then with dairy products and beef (God bless the great state of Wisconsin). I push the cart to the front and Carl surveys my take.

"That will be two hundred and fifty dollars."

Damned inflation. There goes my college fund. Not that I'm going to college anymore. The end of the world really put a pin in my five-year success plan.

I sigh. "Will you take a check?"

"You know I won't," he tells me with a kind smile.

I smile back, showing the teeth, then leaning forward and pressing my elbows together just enough to make it clear that my cleavage is very serious about needing some protein.

He looks. Of course he looks. Beautiful girls in gowns aren't sashaying down these aisles every day. But he also blushes, which is damn decent of him.

"Look, if you pay for the powder and beef, I'll give you the dairy for free."

"Deal!"

"So that will be…two hundred even. Cash or trade only."

"Thanks, Carl!" I throw the bills down on the counter. Before I wheel my cart on out, I ask him the same question I always do. "Hey, uh, any outsiders come through town lately?"

He looks at me with something like pity in his eyes. "Ya know I woulda told you, if I did."

"Right, I know," I lie. The truth is, I'm pretty sure Carl would lie. He thinks my plan to get myself kidnapped in order to save my best friend is suicidal.

"I'll see you next week," I promise him with one last smile and wave.

I keep an eye on the lot as I move out toward my truck. The group I'm looking to have steal me aren't the only villains roaming these streets. These are desperate times. It's best to assume somebody's watching me, wanting to find out what I bought and how hard it would be to take it from me. And if that somebody decides I'm an easy target, they'll attack now—while I'm moving stuff over to my vehicle, no hands free to wield my bat.

I saw a movie once where a secret agent infiltrates a beauty pageant. Her talent is self-defense. I wish I'd made that my talent instead of tap. What, am I going to dance an attacker to death? Although I did take kickboxing down at the Y twice a week, so I know a few moves. Kickboxing burns some damn calories, let me tell you. Also, you could bounce a quarter off my ass after only two months.

"Brandee Jean?" someone says, and I spin around, baseball bat raised, heart pounding with fear.

It's a girl about my age. She's beautiful, with long legs and a heart shaped face. With a little refinement, she could kill it on the pageant circuit. She's also wearing some kind of school girl outfit, from a private school or something. Or a porn film shoot. I hear *that* business is still doing just fine.

"What do you want?" I ask, brandishing the bat.

She smiles, not at all afraid. "My name is Edie and I'm here to take you to Amazon Academy."

I spit out a laugh. "Guuurl, I'm not into that line of work."

I look around to make sure there's no one else lurking nearby. Sometimes they work in groups. One will distract you while someone else steals your stuff.

"I don't want your food," she tells me. "I just need you to listen for a moment…"

I don't let her finish. I get into the truck and hit the gas, giving her a pageant wave as I speed away. The world is crazy enough. I don't need a rando girl talking about academies—whatever that's code for. And given her getup, I'm assuming something slightly south of acceptable.

I watch her grow smaller in the rearview mirror. It looks like she doesn't have a vehicle either, which means she won't be giving chase. That's a relief. My old truck starts to rattle something awful anytime I get over 40mph.

Usually, I can relax a little once I turn onto my street. But as I make the left onto Colby Court, I spot something flying overhead. I immediately pull the truck over, scanning the perfectly blue slice of sky in the rearview mirror.

Is it a helicopter? Is someone coming to restore order and make everything go back to the way it used to be?

I get out, shading my eyes.

Dammit. No, of course not.

It's a stupid dragon up there.

I give the dragon the finger. The world is a messed-up place now. Six months ago, I would've thought I was taking too many diet pills. Or that I just needed a Lunesta and a good long nap.

Now, though, a dragon doesn't even count as the

weirdest thing I've seen lately. Before the news went out, there were reports that vampires are real. And I swear, last month I saw a girl change into a cat and run off.

When I get home, the same girl from the Piggly Wiggly parking lot is waiting on my doorstep. I get out of the truck, bat in hand and ready to swing. I'm not playing right now. This is my property. My safe place. But her being here makes it a lot less safe.

And I hate that.

"How do you know where I live?" I ask, tightening the grip on my bat.

"I Googled you," she tells me with a smirk.

"How did you get here so fast?"

"I flew. And you really didn't need to flip me off," she adds.

I'm about to ask her what in the seven pageant hells she's talking about (circle two is the swimsuit competition), when purple wings sprout out of her back. Crap.

I keep my bat up as I approach her. "*You're* the dragon?"

"Are you ready to listen now?"

I hesitate, weighing the risks and rewards. If this dragon wanted to hurt me, she would've done it already. Unless she's a psychopath dragon who likes to play with her victims first. Either way, she seems determined. I'd rather invite her into my home, than have her go all dragon again and come crashing down through the roof.

"Sure," I say, trying not to look impressed. "If you help me get the groceries inside." My mama taught me that whatever else is going on, keep your priorities on track. Dragon-girl shrugs and grabs a box of Quik Powder.

"And no shoes in the house," I call over my shoulder. I put the food in the icebox and motion for her to sit at the kitchen table. I also make two glasses of Quik Powder as a snack. When I place it in front of her she stares at the mixture like it's roadkill.

"Drink up," I tell her. "That stuff's precious."

"Yes, of course." She takes a hesitant sip.

"So," I eye her. "What do you want with me?"

"Well, here's the thing—god is dead."

"Oh no, are you one of those end-of-the-worlders?" I shake my head. "I'm not joining your dragon cult and sacrificing myself to the flames, or whatever it is you weirdos do. Sorry, but I already got plans to join this 'we keep girls in cages' group next time they come through town recruiting."

She frowns at me. "You want to join a group that plans to put you in a cage?"

"Long story, I'd rather not get into it right now." It's actually not that long of a story, but I don't feel like sharing it with a stranger. "So if your group is looking for some sucker to feed one of their organs to a warlock who promises to roll back time, well sorry, but I'm not voluntarily giving any of them up."

One year, Miss North County Bee Hive Queen donated a kidney, faked appendicitis, and had her uterus removed, all in an effort to lose a few pounds. Her scars totally showed during the bikini competition though. Not worth it.

"There are no warlocks who can turn back time. Probably. Not that I know of. And—" She stops and takes another sip of Quik Powder. "We've gotten off course. Let me start again. *A* god is dead. Zeus, to be exact."

"The lightning bolt guy?"

"Yes. Exactly." She looks relieved. "You know who Mr. Zee, er, Zeus is. At least that's one less thing I have to explain."

"No...I think you still got a lot to explain. But let's start with Zeus. You're telling me he's real and also that he's now dead. And I'm...what? His long-lost daughter set to inherit everything he left behind?"

"Actually..." She hesitates and I see laughter in her eyes. Like she knows this is absurd. "*I'm* his long-lost daughter."

I take a moment to wonder if I got a batch of bad powder and am hallucinating. But, if people accept that vampires are real, and I witnessed this girl—as a dragon—follow me home from the Piggly Wiggly, how much larger a leap is required to accept that the Greek gods are real?

She gives me a sugar-free candy smile. Sweet, but definitely not the real thing. She'd never make it on the beauty queen circuit. "Anyway, after Zeus died, things went to Hades overnight. A bunch of the minor gods went haywire without anybody in charge. There were crazy storms. Earthquakes. Hurricanes. Tornadoes."

"I noticed," I tell her. "Here in Wisconsin we had a blizzard in August. Also, you know, vampires. And"—I give her the side eye just so she knows not to make fun of me when I finish my sentence—"I totally saw a girl turn into a housecat."

"Oh," Edie lights up. "That was my sister, Mavis. With all the chaos in the world, many of us supernatural creatures have been doing what we can to restore the balance. Mavis has been keeping an eye on you for a while."

My side eye still stands. "*Because*?"

"We're pretty sure some of Zeus's powers went to you when he died." She studies me, almost like she's trying to see beneath my skin. "Notice anything weird lately?"

"Oh, I don't know, like maybe that time I got struck by lightning and it didn't kill me?"

Edie leans back in her chair. "Can you walk me through exactly what happened?"

"I was out looking for Bethany Ully—she's Miss All-

Midwest Body Butter. I had a bone to pick with her, on account of I found out she'd been using body wraps to shed some pounds."

"Is that illegal in a pageant?" Edie asks, and I shake my head.

"No, but we'd all made a pact that we were playing it straight for the summer. Strictly self-starving. But I spotted Bethany's name on the sign-in sheet at the Skinned and Tanned—that's a local business that does real well around here. The husband is a taxidermist and the wife is a cosmetologist."

"So they're both into preservation," Edie says, with a wry smile.

"Anyway," I say, waving my hand, "I went in for my bi-weekly tanning bed bake and that's when I saw her big loopy handwriting three slots above mine. She'd been in for a wrap appointment earlier that day." I shake my head, still peeved about it. "Beth didn't even bother covering her tracks. You can be shady or you can be sloppy, but not both. At least that's what my mama taught me. As a friend, I decided to deliver that message to her in person."

"Just a friendly chat?" she asks, raising her eyebrows.

"Not hardly. I was gonna rip out every single one of her new extensions."

"Seriously?" Edie looks disgusted and I wonder if she's some sort of pacifist dragon, but then she adds, "Hair pulling. Slapping. Spitting. That sort of fighting almost seems quaint."

I narrow my eyes at her. "Quaint my ass. She would've had bald patches when I was done with her."

Edie gives a slight nod that almost looks like approval. Not a peace-lover after all, then, I guess.

"So what happened?" Edie asks.

"I stopped home before paying her a visit. I wanted to wear my crown from the Miss Street & Sanitation competition, just to remind her what's what. I was cutting across the high school soccer fields when the first storm whipped up."

"Let me guess," Edie interrupts. "The sky went from bright blue to darkest black in an instant?"

"Out. Of. Nowhere," I confirm. "I made a run for it, but I might as well have had a lightning rod on my head. Took all of three steps before—*WHAM!*"

I smack the table with both hands and Edie jumps.

"Just like that I was on my ass, smelling like a Pop Tart that's been in the toaster too long."

"And...?" Edie prompts me. "Did you notice anything after the lightning strike? Anything unusual?" She's leaning forward, practically salivating.

"Like the fact that I can deadlift three hundred times my own body weight?" I ask, chugging down my Quik Powder and wiping my mouth.

It took me a few weeks to figure that out. At first I was just happy to have survived that lightning strike. Then all the social fabric busted wide open—kinda like when Jenny May Malone dropped her baton at the third annual Miss Midwest Pure Pork Princess and the seams on her dress couldn't continue hiding her five months along baby belly. It wasn't pretty.

I can't remember much of the dark days right after that. Mama was real low and I didn't see the point of pulling her out of it. But then one night she woke me at 3 a.m., all hopped up on something that made the smile on her face look all painful and stretched out. Mama said she'd had a vision that mani-pedis would help pull us through the apocalypse. By the time I pulled on the dress Mama insisted I wear, she was passed out cold. But I figured I'd go and get the nail polishes Mama wanted anyway. Figured it might keep Mama from sinking back down in the darkness...and taking me with her.

I was picking my way across Main Street when an abandoned car rolled onto my evening gown hem. That's when I noticed the not-so-nice guy eyeing me from the alley. Instead of ripping my dress (Dolce & Gabbana, secondhand, $4,500), I tried to lift the car...and succeeded.

I thought it was just the adrenaline, you know, like when a woman goes all mama bear because her baby is in danger? But then when I got back home I did an experiment and flipped the neighbor's RV. So...

"That's not normal," Edie says, grinning.

"I do know that," I tell her. "So fine, if you say I got a bit of Zeus's power or whatever, I believe you."

"Good!" She sits back. "You're honestly way ahead of where I was when I started."

"You still haven't said what you want with me."

"If you want to keep your new power, you have to come with me to Amazon Academy. Once you're there, they'll find out if you can fill the void that was created when Zeus died. A bunch of different people got different pieces of him. We need all of you to compete. One winner will end up with all of Zeus's powers, and he or she can then restore order to the world." She sits back with an 'easy peasy' look on her face.

But I feel like she left out a big piece of the puzzle. "Okay and what about the losers?"

"Oh, um," Edie clears her throat. "If you lose, you lose your powers."

"But you just said I gotta go to this Amazon Academy if I want to *keep* my power!" The words explode out of me, because truth to tell, even though my super strength is still new, it's already become a part of me. Sorta like when you get a new lipstick and immediately realize it's gonna be your new signature color.

Edie holds her hands out in a calm down gesture. "Okay, look. Anyone who doesn't arrive at Amazon Academy by the evening of the opening ceremony will lose their powers. And that's tomorrow."

"Tomorrow!" I take a deep breath, fighting back the growing panic. "So let me get this straight. If I want to stay super strong, I gotta follow you to this Wonder Woman Academy, Hunger Games it out with a bunch of other suddenly supers, and eventually rise to the top?"

"Don't freak out, but"—she reaches across the table and takes my hand—"the other contestants aren't all people. Some are vampires or shifters, like me, and yes, some are humans like you. And there are quite a few royals in the mix."

A sharp laugh escapes me. "Like another pageant queen?"

"Well...no. Royalty by blood," Edie admits.

"So you got stuck with me, a beauty queen? Are they punishing you?"

"No, actually. I chose you."

I bark out a laugh. "You had the option of picking an actual princess or queen or whatever, and you chose me? Aren't I a longshot?" What's wrong with this girl? Mama always said you gotta back a winner, even if you like the loser.

"I'm not going to lie to you. The general consensus is that you're the underdog. But I was once like you. I thought I was normal and then discovered I had incredible power. With my help, I think you can do this. You can be crowned the new Zeus." She pauses. "I'm not explaining this very well, am I?"

"Nah, you're doing just fine. You want me to compete for a crown. If I win, I'll be in charge of the gods."

My heart pounds loud in my chest as I look around the house. Mama wasn't much into decorating, but she always made sure to frame and hang my pageant pictures. From ages five and up, I'm there on the wall, competing for sashes and scepters.

Usually winning meant a crown, a sash, and a cash prize. Most of the money would go to paying for my dresses, the dance choreographer, and dental work. Shiny chompers don't come cheap. Any money left over, Mama would hide in a Ziploc at the back of the freezer. Her not believing in banking institutions is why I still got money to spend.

Some of the bigger pageants cost so much up front that —even though Mama never said it aloud—losing wasn't an option. I always at least placed at those times. Mama always said, "You're a diamond, Brandee Jean. You shine brightest when you're pressed the hardest."

She also said, "Only losers worry about what happens when they lose."

Finally, I turn to Edie, and push my chair back with a screech.

"Girl, I understand perfectly." I stand. "Let me grab my tiara, then we'll go show them what a real queen looks like."

BUY IT NOW!

ALSO BY THE AUTHORS

ANOTHER LITTLE PIECE by Kate Karyus Quinn

FREE with KindleUnlimited for a limited time only!

The spine-tingling horror of Stephen King meets an eerie mystery worthy of Sara Shepard's Pretty Little Liars series in Kate Karyus Quinn's haunting debut.

On a cool autumn night, Annaliese Rose Gordon stumbled out of the woods and into a high school party. She was screaming. Drenched in blood. Then she vanished.

A year later, Annaliese is found wandering down a road hundreds of miles away. She doesn't know who she is. She doesn't know how she got there. She only knows one thing: She is not the real Annaliese Rose Gordon.

Now Annaliese is haunted by strange visions and broken

memories. Memories of a reckless, desperate wish . . . a bloody razor . . . and the faces of other girls who disappeared.

Piece by piece, Annaliese's fractured memories come together to reveal a violent, endless cycle that she will never escape—unless she can unlock the twisted secrets of her past.

CLICK NOW to buy or borrow with KU!

THE SHOW MUST GO ON by Kate Karyus Quinn

While You Were Sleeping meets *Pitch Perfect* in this hilarious romantic comedy that will have you laughing—and singing along too.

Jenna is certain of three things:

1. No way is she already thirty years old.

   (Except...she is.)

2. *Annie* the musical should never be crossed with *Fifty Shades of*

Grey.

(But this perfectly describes the show she's currently starring in.)

and

3. She can never return home—even if after twelve years her ex-boyfriend, Danny, wakes up from his coma and asks for her by name.

(Which he does.)

Okay, so sometimes Jenna gets a few things wrong. But she's definitely sticking with her never going home plan. (At least until Danny's younger brother, Will, arrives on Jenna's doorstep and insists on escorting her back to Buffalo, NY—and Danny's bedside.)

Fine. Maybe Jenna can go home again. But she's not staying.

And she's definitely not falling in love.

(Right?)

For fans of Sally Thorne, Penny Reid, and Lucy Parker, this standalone chick lit novel will give you all the feels.

FREE with KindleUnlimited!

————

IN THE AFTER by Demitria Lunetta

Perfect for fans of *The 5th Wave* and *A Quiet Place*.

Amy Harris's life changed forever when They took over. Her parents—vanished. The government—obsolete. Societal structure —nonexistent. No one knows where They came from, but these vicious creatures have been rapidly devouring mankind since They appeared.

With fierce survivor instincts, Amy manages to stay alive—and even rescues "Baby," a toddler who was left behind. After years of hiding, they are miraculously rescued and taken to New Hope. On the surface, it appears to be a safe haven for survivors. But there are dark and twisted secrets lurking beneath that could have Amy and Baby paying with not only their freedom . . . but also their lives.

BUY NOW

———

DOWN WITH THE SHINE by Kate Karyus Quinn

Only $1.99

Think twice before you make a wish in this imaginative, twisted, and witty new novel from the author of *Another Little Piece*.

When Lennie brings a few jars of her uncles' moonshine to Michaela Gordon's house party, she has everyone who drinks it make a wish. It's tradition. So is the toast her uncles taught her: "May all your wishes come true, or at least just this one."

The thing is, those words aren't just a tradition. The next morning, every wish—no matter how crazy—comes true. And most of them turn out bad. But once granted, a wish can't be unmade . . .

BUY NOW

———

AMONG THE SHADOWS: Thirteen Stories of Darkness & Light

Available through KindleUnlimited!

Edited and with stories written by Demitria Lunetta and Kate Karyus Quinn

Even the lightest hearts have shaded corners to hide the black thoughts that come at night. Experience the darker side of YA as 13 authors explore the places that others prefer to leave among the shadows.

BUY NOW

———

BETTY BITES BACK

FEMINIST FICTION TO FRIGHTEN THE PATRIARCHY!

Available through KindleUnlimited!

Edited and with stories written by Demitria Lunetta and Kate Karyus Quinn

Behind every successful man is a strong woman... but in these stories, she might be about to plant a knife in his spine. The characters in this anthology are fed up - tired of being held back, held down, held accountable - by the misogyny of the system. They're ready to resist by biting back in their own individual ways, be it through magic, murder, technology, teeth, pitfalls and even... potlucks. Join sixteen writers as they explore feminism in fantasy, science-fiction, fractured fairy-tales, historical settings, and the all-too-familiar chauvinist contemporary world.

BUY NOW

ABOUT THE AUTHORS

DEMITRIA LUNETTA is the author of the YA books THE FADE, BAD BLOOD, and the sci-fi duology, IN THE AFTER and IN THE END. She is also an editor and contributing author for the YA anthology, AMONG THE SHADOWS: 13 STORIES OF DARKNESS & LIGHT. Find her at www.demitrialunetta.com for news on upcoming projects and releases.

KATE KARYUS QUINN is an avid reader and menthol chapstick addict with a BFA in theater and an MFA in film and television production. She lives in Buffalo, New York with her husband, three children, and one enormous dog. She has three young adult novels published with HarperTeen: ANOTHER LITTLE PIECE, (DON'T YOU) FORGET ABOUT ME, AND DOWN WITH THE SHINE. She also recently released her first adult novel, THE SHOW MUST GO ON, a romantic comedy. Find out more at www.katekaryusquinn.com

MARLEY LYNN is a lost child of the gods, who waits on the shores of Lake Erie for her parents to bring her home. In the meantime, she contents herself with reading, writing, and gardening. Find out more at www.MarleyLynn.com

ACKNOWLEDGMENTS

Thank you to Marin McGinnis for taking care of our copy edits!

Thank you to our cover designer Victoria @VC_BookCovers

And, of course, a big thank you to our families for putting up with us crazy writers.

CPSIA information can be obtained
at www.ICGtesting.com
Printed in the USA
LVHW031937301120
673038LV00024B/1402